KILLINGTIME

JOHN PENNEY

Encyclopocalypse Publications www.encyclopocalypse.com

ONE

Her muffled screams were swallowed up by the flickering night sounds of the black water Atchafalaya Swamp. There was no one around for miles to hear her.

From the outside, the only sign of the desperate struggle going on inside the old Toyota parked on the deserted road behind the Camaro was the silent shadowy movement in the back seat. Inside was a different story.

Inside, the struggle was loud, frantic and desperate; she was fighting for her life. His rough hands were cold and sticky as they slapped hard against her bare breast. His breath reeked of stale tobacco and beer. It was a violent and ugly act. She fought back as best she could, clawing her nails into his thick forearm as he ripped open the other side of her blouse and tore away her bra. She felt his penis slap against her inner thigh. His free hand groped for her panties. He was getting close to entering her now, and she knew she had to do something.

She swung her free foot against the side window as hard as she could. Out of the corner of her eye, she saw the glass fragment into the shape of tiny ice cubes. She kicked again. The glass dented out slightly. She looked back up at his sweating face. She screamed.

WHAP! He slapped his hand over her wet mouth. She tasted the salt and tobacco from his dirty fingers on her tongue. Every instinct was telling her that she should clench her mouth tightly closed. But she didn't. Instead, she opened her mouth wide; the side of his hand slipped in and she bit down with all her might.

He cried out and yanked his hand away. Blood sprayed over the dirty upholstery from his tattered fingers. The fist of his other hand slammed hard into her rib cage. She heard a sickening crack as her bone gave way. For a split second, she couldn't breathe.

He sat back, clutching his bleeding hand. This was going to be her only chance, and she knew it.

She caught her breath and jerked her knee upward, crushing his balls into his swollen penis. He let out a guttural groan, recoiled, and released her. She clawed for the door handle, yanked it down, and bolted out of the car.

Her bare feet slapped down onto the clammy asphalt; she tugged up her blood-splattered shorts. WHAM! The car door burst open behind her, and the big man's flailing body tumbled out. This was far from over.

He was coming for her.

She cut around the Camaro parked behind her Toyota, then ran down the embankment and into the bayou. It was a shadowy jungle of bald cypress trees draped with long beard-like moss; a dense mist hugged the stale water.

Adrenaline pushed her body forward. She ignored whatever it was that squished between her toes in the mucky bottom. She was eighteen, toned, and in good shape. He was drunk and out of shape; there was a good chance she could get away as long as she kept running.

She had made it several yards into the water when she slipped down a small ledge and found herself up to her waist. She regained her balance and looked back through the heavy mist; she could see that he was as determined as she was. He was steadily gaining on her.

She wrenched around and pushed herself forward, sloshing through the black water. Something sharp stabbed her foot—a shell? A broken bottle?—and she cried out. The floor of the bayou began to rise again as she reached the other bank. She saw a dilapidated boathouse built on stilts out over the edge of the swamp. She splashed her way over, pulled herself up onto the deck, yanked open the old door, and darted inside.

In the shadowy dark, she could see that the shack was strewn with beer cans left from teen-age partiers; there was graffiti painted on the walls and a tattered mattress in the corner next to a pile of rusted boat parts. She closed the door behind her, frantically searched through the old boat parts, and found a broken propeller. It was an awkward weapon, but the edges were sharp, and she could defend herself with it. She crept back over to the door and pressed herself against the wall. She steadied her breathing and listened. The sloshing sound of a person striding purposefully through water came to her and grew louder.

She swallowed dryly and raised the propeller high, poised to strike when he entered. The sloshing sounds stopped. The soft sound of rippling water lapped against the old boathouse stilts. But then there was nothing else.

She turned around and peered out a crack between two planks in the wall. Her young eyes searched in each direction as far as they could in the dark. The bayou was still and empty. No sign of the man.

Her mind began to race. This couldn't be. He had just been out there. She had heard him coming straight for her through the water. She had heard the waves from the movement of his legs hit the boathouse. He had to know she was hiding in here.

She looked back at the door next to her and decided she didn't have a choice. She had to stick to her original plan. He was coming, and when he came through the door, she would bring the sharp propeller down on him with all her might.

She waited a moment longer. Still nothing. A minute passed, then another. Her arms began to tremble under the weight of the propeller. Where was he? Could he have gone past the boathouse? Maybe he hadn't seen her go in. The questions began to race through her mind. The propeller grew heavier by the second.

She grimaced, lowered the propeller, and took a deep breath. She started to raise it again. CRACK! The rotten wall behind her burst open. A large knife shot out of the darkness; the blade grazed the base of her neck.

Her blood-curdling scream echoed out across the misty, hot swamp. The frogs and crickets, which had created the flickering, unnerving noise of the night, fell silent for a moment, but then they rose again and continued their eternal sound, indifferent to the fate of the young woman in the boathouse.

TWO

THE STERILE ELECTRONIC voice buzzed in Daniel Nash's ear. "You have two new messages. Press one to listen to your message playback."

Daniel's calloused thumb pressed the keypad on the old flip phone, then he raised it to his ear. The three-day stubble on his face scratched against the phone as he listened. He concentrated, trying to block out the loud wind that thumped in through the open window of his Super Duty Ford pickup as he cruised down the Louisiana highway.

"First unheard message..."

An older man's voice with a Texas drawl crackled over the line. "Daniel? This is Art Larson, your landlord back here in Houston. I got the key you dropped off, thanks. Listen, you got a few days of mail here and you didn't leave a forwarding address. Give me a call and let me know where you want them sent. I can also send along your cleaning deposit. So, well, give me a call."

Daniel sighed. There was nothing back there he wanted, no matter what it might be. He looked out through the bug-splattered windshield at the road that stretched in front of him. There were old mud roosters on the hood and a healthy coating of dust over the whole truck. All were signs of the three days he'd been on the road.

Daniel was the perfect match for his truck. He hadn't washed in three days either, or bothered to change his sweat stained T-shirt or his dusty jeans. But if anyone could pull this look off, it was Daniel. Most women he met saw only his strong good looks, blonde hair and his piercing blue eyes; he was the early 30s rugged blue-collar Texas specimen of their fantasies.

The phone beeped again in his ear, and the second message began. It was a crisp woman's voice. "Mr. Nash, this is the Houston Oncology Center regarding the past-due bill for your wife, Angie Nash. We're going to need you to resubmit the bill to your insurance company. They are refusing payment for the balance of the chemotherapy. If you could please call...."

Daniel's thumb angrily stabbed the "end" button, and he snapped the phone closed. He drove for a moment in silence, wrestling with an overwhelming urge to scream a million choice words at the heartless bitch on the phone. He knew who she was. He'd met her at the front desk every time he had gone with Angie for her treatment. All those times, she had spoken to them with concern and caring. It had been a mirage, just like the promise that they could beat the lymphoma. Daniel had lost the only woman he ever loved, and the people who couldn't save her were now hounding him for money. Fucking vultures.

Daniel took a cleansing breath and glanced into the dirty rear-view mirror. Everything he had in the world was in this truck-and it wasn't much. There was a duffle bag of clothes and a pair of extra work boots, a cooler of food so he could keep driving, and, of course, a full complement of his construction tools. They were his lifeline. His saving grace. They were the only things that had kept him sane during the hellish days while Angie was deteriorating.

Daniel had found solace in his work, in the simple satisfaction of crafting wood into something new—building a place that was solid and sound for people to live in for generations. His mind often leaped to lofty ambitions like that; carpentry had never been just a way to make a living. It was his art. Of course, when he had been back in Houston growing up, he would never have been able to tell any of his fellow construction workers his feelings on the subject. He knew better. They were a different breed—get a job done and go on to the next one, with no thought about having created a place where a family would live its life. But their views didn't matter to Daniel. Carpentry was something special to him, and he had shared his feelings about it only with Angie.

It seemed strange to look back on a life that had peaked and vanished so quickly. He had lost everything he had ever wanted—a woman he loved, and a passion for his work. The loss made him feel unstuck, with nothing much holding him anywhere in particular. When the job opportunity had come up in Louisiana, he had no reason not to take it. It would give him time alone with his work again. He would, he hoped, rediscover the passion he had lost.

The cell phone was the last thread that connected him to everything behind him. He pondered it in his hand for a moment, then tossed it out the open window.

The old phone shattered into a dozen pieces on the warm asphalt of the highway that ran along the Atchafalaya River. A car passing in the other direction ran over it, scattering the plastic pieces. Daniel watched some of them until they came to rest beneath a sign that read "Krotz Springs, 12 Miles."

———

Daniel slowed his truck on the narrow county road and turned into a muddy driveway, past a rusting mailbox that was stenciled with the faded name "Waynright". He squinted through his dirty windshield into the low-lying sun that flickered through the forest of bald cypress as he made his way through the hot, soggy bayou land.

He rounded the driveway's final curve, and the once-proud Waynright house came into view. It was two stories, with an expansive front porch and a large barn nearby. Not too bad. He expected it to be much more run down, based on the conversations he'd had about it with the architect. Aside from the overgrown yard and peeling paint, the old place looked structurally sound. It had good bones.

A new Mercedes was parked in the driveway, and a flashy young couple in expensive casual clothes was talking to a middle-aged Asian woman on the front porch who was holding a roll of blueprints. That had to be Eileen Cho.

Cho was the architect who had hired Daniel to renovate this house. She had short, graying hair with tips that had been dyed purple, and she wore a colorful blouse and black tights. Definitely the creative type he expected her to be, but much older than she had sounded on the phone.

Cho broke into a broad smile and waved as Daniel pulled to a stop. He shut off the truck and stepped out, stiffly unfolding his legs and twisting his back to loosen up a bit.

"Mr. Nash?" Cho said, as she stepped to the edge of the porch.

"Daniel," he said, as he approached with his hand extended. Cho took his hand and shook it, then turned to the over-dressed couple behind her on the porch.

"This is Pat and Samantha Miles. Our homeowners."

"Nice to meet you," Daniel nodded.

"I found Daniel through an architect friend in Houston," Cho explained.

Pat came over and gave Daniel a hearty handshake "Pleasure to meet you, Daniel." His grip was firm and solid, a detail that belied his metro-sexual preppy vibe. Probably trying to overcompensate, Daniel thought. Daniel tried to make eye contact with the young wife, but she looked away, with a vague smile on her thin, pretty face. Daniel had seen a lot of her type growing up in Houston, blonde and over-groomed—the kind who had been told all her life how beautiful she was.

Daniel was aware of how he looked to her, and he said impulsively, "Fresh off the road, not lookin' my best, sorry." As soon as the words were out, Daniel felt unhappy with himself; why the fuck did he have to explain himself to her?

Cho plowed right past the awkward moment. "Pat and Samantha have a plane back to Memphis in a few hours. We were just about to go inside."

"Lead on." Daniel smiled, feeling his old confidence returning, and he climbed the steps. He followed them across the porch, where Cho unlocked the front door.

It was dark in the living room, and Cho snapped on the overhead light. It wasn't what Daniel expected. The furniture and possessions had all been left behind. The larger pieces were covered with drop cloths, but grimy figurines still stood on tables and dusty books leaned on shelves. Little had been touched here for at least ten years.

Cho had told Daniel that the family had abandoned the house a decade ago and there had been nothing done with it since then. It was a detail Daniel hadn't given much thought to at the time and never pressed Cho to explain, but now that he was seeing it first hand with all the belongings in place, it struck him as odd and somewhat eerie.

Cho marched over to the dining area, which adjoined the living room. She slipped the rubber bands off the roll of blueprints and spread the sheets out on the covered dining room table in front of the group. Daniel pulled open the heavy, dust-filled drapes to let more light inside.

Cho jumped into her spiel. She tapped on a section of the blueprint and gestured to the entryway they had just come through. "Opening up the entryway to the living room and removing that kitchen wall will give this room the open-flow energy you guys were looking for," she said. She pointed to the enclosed staircase that led to the second floor "And once we open the staircase up, it should naturally pull that energy upward."

Wow. She really was full of New Age bullshit, Daniel thought, as he smiled and nodded politely. He had gotten an earful of her feng shui theories on remodeling and design over the phone. Most of the time, he had had to talk her down into specifics. Specifics—those were the things Daniel needed to know about. Things like which walls were load-bearing, and what kind of support beams he would need to add. He thought for sure once that he met her she'd drop the act. But here she was, at it again, and the newlyweds were lapping it up.

Pat kissed Samantha on the cheek excitedly. "I'm really loving this, honey," he said. Then he gushed to Cho, "I gotta admit, all this talk about energy flow didn't make a lick of sense to me at first, but now...wow, it's hard to argue with the results. Brilliant stuff, Cho."

Cho started to the stairs and the couple followed her like puppies. "Thanks, but you know, it's funny. Sometimes I think it's hard to call them my ideas. What I try to do is tune into the space and feel what it's telling me. You know, try to discover its potential. The real trick is not trying to move the wrong wall or remove the wrong window. Doing that can throw off a room's energy.

"Like I said, I don't get it, but I like it!" Pat laughed.

Daniel smiled again to himself as he followed them up the stairs. Cho really had them drinking her New Age Kool Aid for sure. When Daniel was younger, he would have probably called them all on the bullshit, but not now. Now, it didn't really matter what of any of them said, as long as their checks cleared and they left him alone to do his work.

Upstairs, as they trooped down the dark, dingy hallway, Pat looked back at Daniel. "Eileen says you'll be staying here during the remodel."

"That's the plan," Daniel replied, surprised the man even remembered that he was with them.

"Great. We'd heard some of the local kids from Krotz Springs like to come down this way to party. It'll be great have someone around all the time."

"No worries. Your place'll be just fine. My partyin' days are long over," Daniel reassured him.

Cho stopped at a dingy pink door at the end of the hall. She turned the knob and gave a shove, but the old door was stuck. Daniel stepped forward. "Lemme see," he said.

Daniel turned the knob firmly and leaned into the door. No luck. He reared back and slammed his shoulder into it. Still no luck. The pink door was sealed tight.

"Wow. Gonna have to take my Sawzall to this puppy, for sure," Daniel said, and gave it a final smack.

"It's all right, Daniel. We don't need to get in there now," Cho said as she pointed to the inner wall and looked back at the newly-weds. "From here on back, we're going to open this side of the hallway and join it with the bedroom on the other side. It'll create one large second bedroom." She went back down the hallway with the young wife.

Pat followed with Daniel. "It's in amazing shape, huh?" Pat said. "I mean, considering it's been empty all these years." He shot a look at the stained ceiling. "You think any of this old Katrina damage is a problem?"

Daniel looked up at the discolored ceiling. The damage had

probably started long before the hurricane. "Not a problem I can't fix," he said, smiling at Pat. "It's what I do."

Pat slapped Daniel on the back. "Now that's the kind of answer I like. You know, if you're ever in the market for a Porsche, come on up to Memphis, and I'll hook you up."

A Porsche dealer from Memphis. Of course. Now it all made sense, Daniel thought. The overpriced clothes, the manicured hands. All great for presentation, but not long on substance. Now it all fit together. Pat was a car salesman. A good one, but still a car salesman.

They all filed into the large master bedroom at the other end of the hall. It was a generous size, and it took up an entire corner of the house. Again, furniture was draped with dust covers. Cho pulled aside the heavy curtains. "Here," she said, "the wall on the master bath will push back to the hall wall." She turned back to the main room. "As we discussed, opening the windows over there and placing your bed here," she motioned to a spot opposite the covered double bed that sat forlornly against a wall, "will give this room the space and at the same time give it that intimate, sexual energy you were looking for."

Daniel glanced over and saw the young wife discreetly squeeze her car-dealing husband's ass. "I can feel it already," she purred into his ear.

Daniel looked away. Did she really just do that? It took every bit of self-restraint he could muster not to roll his eyes.

———

An hour later, the young couple were in the back seat of Cho's Mercedes, and Cho and Daniel strolled from the house toward the car.

"Cute couple, aren't they?" Cho winked at Daniel.

"Adorable," Daniel replied. They shared a private, sardonic smile, then they both gave a little laugh.

"The estate executor said he'd try to have all the furniture and personal stuff out of the house some time next week," she said. "Can you work around it for now?"

"Shouldn't be a problem. Just call and give me a heads up. Oh, I've got a new number. Daniel took out a new disposable phone and checked the display "It's 662..."

"Can you text it to me?"

"Sure. Okay."

They reached the Mercedes. Cho tossed the blueprints into the passenger seat, then turned back and took Daniel's hand, "It was nice to meet you face to face. I'm really glad you agreed to take this job."

Daniel nodded and started to pull his hand away, but she held him tighter.

"I know you think all my rambling about destiny is silly, but I really do think this was meant to be." There was something sincere and real about Cho as she looked at him now. As odd as he thought she was, he couldn't dismiss her so easily. It was clear she was feeling something, but was it something about the job? Or something about him?

Daniel softened and smiled. "Hey, whatever works. I'll take a job any way I can get it."

The moment between them lasted a bit longer, then she laughed and pushed away from him. "All right, all right. I know how I sound sometimes." She opened her car door, then looked back at him. "But I'm not usually wrong about things like this."

"Have a safe drive back to the city," Daniel smiled.

"Don't forget to text me your new number."

Daniel held up his phone. "Doing it right now."

Cho started the Mercedes and pulled away. Daniel dialed

Cho and entered his number in a text. When he looked back up, the Mercedes was gone.

Daniel stood for a moment alone in the front yard. The morning sounds of the bayou seemed muffled by the muggy warmth that surrounded him. He scanned the rustic surroundings. The bayou seemed to be encroaching on the property. The twisting branches of the dark trees and the dangling moss looked like they were slowly strangling the dilapidated barn and the rutted driveway.

Then it hit him. He was all alone out here except for the singing cicadas, miles from town in the middle of the Atchafalaya Basin. He turned, pushed through the rusted wrought iron gate, and started back up to the house. He stepped onto the porch and paused again. He looked into the front door. It was dark inside.

He was about to take another step, when out of nowhere an anxious feeling crept deep into his bones. What was he really doing here? Was this just a job that had come his way through a random connection with Cho's architect friend in Houston? Or was there more to it? How had Cho found this house? What had happened to the people who owned it, and why had all their belongings been left here for more than a decade? It wasn't like other remodeling jobs he'd had, where the houses had been cleared of personality and he could concentrate on making them ready for a new family and new memories. Here, there was a residue of the former owners—a mysterious sense of something unfinished, of questions unanswered.

Since Angie's death, Daniel had been feeling strangely disconnected. Everything that had tied him to one place in the world had been taken from him, so he had floated along day after day until now—until he found himself standing on the porch of this deserted house that seemed to be protecting its forgotten possessions from some of the eeriest swampland in the world.

Daniel forced himself to take a shallow breath. Maybe it was all of Cho's talk about energy flow and fate that was making him feel this way.

He took a second breath. Deeper this time. Then another. That was better. Breathe. That's all he had to do. Breathe. He managed to push the feelings out of his head. He still had a lot of daylight ahead of him. He could get started.

THREE

It was almost noon when Daniel came into the small guest room off the kitchen and snapped on the light. The guest room was as old and dingy as the rest of the house. There was a small single bed and a half-bath attached. Back when the house was in its glory, this had been intended as a housekeeper's apartment. It had been largely ignored and used mostly for storage in the intervening decades. But it was small and simple and would be the perfect place for Daniel to camp out while he dismantled the rest of the house.

He stripped the dust cover off of the bed and wadded it into a corner of the kitchen. Then he tossed his duffle bag of clothes and his sleeping bag on the bed, which was, happily, made up with linen and a light blanket, and walked back out to the kitchen. He opened the cooler, which he had refilled with beer and ready-made sandwiches at the Wal-Mart where he had bought the new disposable cell phone out on the highway. He got one out and ripped off the plastic, ate half of it in a couple of bites, then rewrapped it and put it back in the cooler. He wanted to get started.

He grabbed his large toolbox off the counter and carried it into the living room. He set it down with a heavy thump on the old coffee table, then threw open the lid and took out a can of red spray paint. He grabbed a reduced copy of the blueprints, reviewed them for a moment, and crossed over to the entryway wall. He spray-painted a large "X" across the entire wall, then moved to the kitchen wall and sprayed another large "X." He paused a moment in the shaft of light that streamed in through the front window and consulted the blueprints for the other walls that had to be demolished.

The shimmering sound of the cicadas outside swelled loudly, then receded into abrupt silence. At the same time, the musty living room became dead and airless. Daniel froze in his tracks. The anxious feeling crept back over him like a heavy weight being pressed deep into his chest. He tried to inhale but came up short. It was as if something were pulling the breath out of his lungs. The world began to spin. Daniel closed his eyes, concentrated, and forced a deep breath.

He opened his eyes, and a shadow passed over the blueprints in his hand.

Daniel shot a look at the front window, but there was no one there.

He stared at the window for a moment as his eyes adjusted and his mind started to race. Someone had walked past on the porch outside and had cast that shadow. Or maybe the person was inside. It had to be one of the other.

Or did it? Maybe a cloud had passed over the sun.

After a moment, the cicadas started their song outside again. The world returned to normal. Shit. He was anxious. It had to be one of those spells, like the ones he had had when Angie was first diagnosed. It had been a while since he had one; he didn't even have any Xanax to take. Daniel tucked the blueprints under his arm and crossed to the staircase.

The old steps creaked under his weight as he ascended to the second floor. He paused again in the long, dark hallway and consulted the blueprints once more. He shifted them around, orienting the design, then stepped up to the inside wall and sprayed another long "X."

He continued down the hall to the faded pink door and shook the spray can. He raised it, about to paint another "X" on the wall next to it. The wooden stairs creaked behind him.

Daniel froze, then turned and looked back down the long hall. He waited in the silence of the house, listening. He hadn't imagined that sound. Then it happened again. The old wooden steps creaked with the same heavy sound he had made when he walked up them moments earlier.

"Hello?" He waited for whoever was approaching to answer.

There was no response.

Daniel lowered the paint can and started back down the hall. It had to be one of the local kids who had come by and found the front door open, he thought, but when he reached the head of the stairs, the stairwell was empty.

Daniel paused a moment, puzzled, then raised his voice and tried again. "Hello?"

Nothing. No answer.

"Shit," Daniel exhaled. This was going to be a long remodel if he didn't get a grip on himself. He turned away and started back down the hall, shaking the paint can.

He didn't see the long shadow stretch up the stairwell behind him.

Daniel spray-painted another "X" across the wall and pulled out his blueprints as he turned again.

The silhouette was right in front of him.

Daniel recoiled and dropped the can. "Jesus fuck!"

At the same instant, the silhouette leaped back into the partial light. It was an African-American man in his late 20s with a terrified look on his handsome, boyish face. "Damn, dude," he said. "Sorry."

Daniel's heart hammered in his chest. "What the hell do you think you're doing?" he snapped angrily.

"Right now I'm shittin' my pants," the young man offered simply.

Daniel regained his equilibrium; his mind slowed, and he then realized who the man was. "Reggie. You're Reggie, right?"

"Yeah, man. That's me" said the young man. "Damn, you're jumpy."

"I thought I heard something before, and there wasn't anybody, and..." Daniel felt silly and gave up trying to explain himself. "Yeah, I'm jumpy," he admitted. He breathed out and extended his hand. "I'm Daniel. Thanks for comin'."

"No problem," Reggie said, as he shook Daniel's hand.

"I thought you were starting tomorrow."

"Today's the 16th, right?"

"Is it?"

"Yeah, dude. It's the 16th."

"Well then, I guess you're here when you're supposed to be."

"I am."

Daniel reached down and picked up the spray paint can. "I was just marking out the walls we're gonna demo. Come on, you can start downstairs."

Daniel descended the stairs and Reggie followed, looking around at the old place as they went. "Always wondered what the inside of this old place looked like," Reggie said. "Used to party out in the woods near here back in the day."

"Yeah, I've heard this side of the basin is a regular party central for the locals," said Daniel. "You live close by?"

"No one lives close by. That's the point. I grew up about seven miles down the road. Seven miles, but a whole different neighborhood," Reggie answered, emphasizing the word "whole," as they entered the living room.

Daniel noticed a couple of toolboxes by the front door. "That your gear?"

"That's them. You said on the phone you were gonna pay me for a kit rental, right?"

"Depends on what you got."

They crossed over to the toolboxes. Reggie kneeled down and opened them both. Inside was a collection of beautifully kept tools. Daniel pulled out a framing hammer and nodded his approval. "Damn nice," he said honestly.

"Hoping to work for myself some day," Reggie smiled proudly.

Daniel sifted through the tools, quickly taking an inventory in his head. "Looks like you got what you need here. Fifty a day be okay?"

"Fifty? Dude, what do you think those are in there?"

Daniel lifted the top tray in one of the boxes and looked through the tools underneath "Yeah, well, the thing is that I've got most of what we need already."

"Can you do sixty?"

Daniel set the top tray down and flipped the lid closed. "Fifty is as high as I can go, and even that's not in my budget."

Reggie studied Daniel, taking in his dirty T-shirt and frayed jeans. Whoever this guy from Texas was, he sure wasn't doing this to get rich. Reggie shrugged. "Fuck it. Yeah, I'll take fifty."

"Good." Daniel crossed over to the coffee table, grabbed his Sawzall, and continued back to the stairs. "And I'm only payin' you for half a day today. It's almost twelve thirty. Our day starts at seven sharp from now on." He disappeared up the stairs.

Reggie opened his mouth to protest but thought better of it. He shook his head, then grabbed his tool belt and strapped it on.

———

Upstairs, Daniel approached the faded pink door at the end of the hall. This time he paused and looked more closely at the door's surface. It was covered with faded remnants of Pokemon stickers, and he could also see what looked like the yellowing plastic of glow-in-the-dark star stickers. So, despite the pink paint, the room wasn't a nursery. It had probably been a young kid's room, maybe a girl's. He gave the knob another try and pushed inward, even though he knew it was pointless. Sure enough, it was sealed tight.

He found a nearby wall plug, unwound the Sawzall cord, and plugged it in, hoping Cho had turned on the electricity in the old place like he had told her to do. He pulled on his safety goggles, stepped back up to the door, and slid the jagged blade into the doorjamb. He squeezed the saw trigger, and the aggressive blade rattled to life, violently shredding the doorjamb. He moved the blade down into the lock, and the saw churned through that too. The rest of the way to the floor was easier, and he pulled the blade out and shut it down. He stepped back and gave a hard kick.

The door swung open.

Daniel peered in. It was dark and musty like the rest of the house. He pulled off his goggles and stepped inside. Once his eyes adjusted, more details came into focus. Here, there were no dust covers. There was a single pink bed arrayed with Beanie Babies and stuffed animals, a dresser with jewelry hanging from the mirror, a vanity with a dust-covered make-up box and hairbrushes and combs still lying out. Several sealed boxes were stacked in the middle of the room. Everything was coated with ten years' worth of dust. Daniel crossed the room and pulled back the musty pink curtains, which crumbled in his hand. The pale light from outside cut through the heavy coating of dust.

He paused for a moment, as the now-familiar anxious feeling crept up on him once more. The air seemed dense here, much more so than the air in the living room or hallway had been.

Daniel was able to push the smothering feeling out of his

mind much more quickly this time, now that he had decided it was just his anxiety. He looked over at the wall he was going to knock down. There was a faded U2 poster next to a Madonna poster. Abandoned just like the belongings downstairs. Nothing here that he had to preserve. This was going to be easy.

The next couple of hours went rather quickly. Daniel worked upstairs blowing out the hallway wall to the pink room, then moved onto the master bedroom. Reggie worked downstairs opening the entryway and the kitchen wall. It was hot, dusty work, and they both breathed through bandannas and dripping sweat.

Daniel's mind lightened as the day wore on. The work was good for him. This was all beginning to feel familiar. Demolition always made it look like the job was going quickly. Tearing things down was fun.

By late in the afternoon, the humidity was much more intense than Daniel had expected. He was up on a stepladder clearing the loose plaster from the ceiling with his hammer when he had had enough. He needed a drink. Something better than water. He set the hammer on top of the ladder and climbed down.

Downstairs, he passed Reggie, who was jacked into his iPod as he finished the entryway wall.

Daniel pulled open his cooler in the kitchen and took out one of the beers he had bought after he had dumped out the remainder of the food he had carried with him from Houston. He cracked it open and took a long drink. The icy brew went down easily. It was exactly what he needed.

He stepped back into the living room, and Reggie looked up. Daniel raised his beer, pointed to the cooler, and mouthed exaggeratedly, "Help yourself."

Reggie said something that was muffled under his bandanna, then continued working.

Daniel went back upstairs and into the master bedroom. He

set his beer on the floor beneath the ladder and started to climb. He reached the third rung and stopped.

His hammer was missing.

Daniel looked down at the rubble on the floor. No sign of the hammer. "What the fuck," Daniel muttered, annoyed. He climbed back down, kicked through the rubble. Nothing. No hammer.

Daniel went back downstairs. Reggie was barely visible through a cloud of plaster dust as Daniel crossed back through the living room.

Daniel checked the cooler in the kitchen. No hammer. He checked the nearby table and counter. Nothing.

Daniel crossed back out to the living room, annoyed. "Hey!" he yelled. Reggie didn't hear him over the Sawzall and his iPod.

Daniel cut around in front of him. "Reggie!"

Reggie shut off the saw and pulled off his bandanna. "What's up?"

"You see my hammer?"

"Your hammer? No."

"You sure?"

"Yeah, I'm sure. Weren't you using it upstairs?"

"I was, then I came down, and I might have left it in the kitchen, or—-you didn't just pick up a hammer from anywhere down here?"

"No." Reggie patted the hammer in his tool belt. "Got my own, remember? I'm chargin' you for it." He yanked the bandanna back over his face and went back to sawing.

Daniel gave a cursory look around the living room and climbed back up the stairs. It had to have fallen in the rubble under the ladder. It was the only place it could be. He took another swig of his beer as he reached the master bedroom, where he stopped cold.

The hammer was back on the top of the ladder, in plain sight.

What the fuck? Daniel lowered his beer and stepped up to the ladder. He reached up and grabbed the hammer.

What part of this had his mind skipped over? He briefly considered the beer bottle before dismissing it; this was his first of the day, and he was used to a whole hell of a lot more than that.

He looked back at the hammer in his hand. The motherfucker hadn't been there when he came back from the kitchen. That was a fact. But what did it mean? Daniel's mind began to race. Was he losing it?

Daniel considered going back downstairs and saying something to Reggie. But what? What would he say?

Daniel sighed. It was hotter than shit. He was tired. It wasn't the first time in his life that he had lost something and found it where he didn't expect to. It happened to everyone. He decided to ignore it. Like it never happened. What else could he do?

Daniel climbed back up on the ladder and continued clearing the rafters with the hammer. It wasn't long before he found himself lulled back into complacency.

There was no way he could have known that the temporary disappearance of his hammer was the first sign that his life was about to take a sudden dark turn.

FOUR

THE FADING daylight glowed in the sky over the bayou as Reggie climbed into his pickup truck. It had been a good half day's work. Daniel stood on the porch wiping the sweat and plaster dust off his T-shirt. "Seven sharp, right?" he asked Reggie.

"I'll be here," Reggie said as he started up his truck.

"Thanks for a good first day," Daniel added. It wasn't an afterthought; Daniel meant it. Reggie seemed like a good, hard-working guy. He had finished the main demolition downstairs and hadn't complained or mentioned the heat or the dust. He hadn't even accepted a beer because he was worried about using the power tools, then about driving. Conscientous. This was going to work out fine, Daniel thought, as he watched Reggie wave good-bye and rumble off down the muddy driveway.

Daniel stood for a moment in the gathering darkness. The cicadas were silent, and the night sounds of the bayou were starting. Frogs and crickets, by the sound of them. But Daniel didn't know. This was far from the likes of Texas, and that was just fine with him. He was here to do a job, and he was happy to be drifting through the hours of the day, slowly killing time. After a few minutes of listening to the strange night sounds, which were loud, but not as intense as the cicadas, he turned and went back inside.

Daniel pushed through the frosted plastic tarp that covered the newly opened entryway and crossed through the living room; he paused a moment, surveying the changes to the house. The entire entryway and the wall to the kitchen were gone, and the dust-covered furniture had been pushed into the center of the large living room space. There were still piles of debris that needed to be removed, but that could be done in the morning. Daniel strolled into the kitchen, grabbed another beer out of the cooler, and cracked it open. He found the other half of the sandwich he had eaten for lunch and unwrapped the plastic. He wandered back through the living room and climbed the stairs.

It was getting too dark to see anything when he reached the hallway and clicked on the overhead light. The light bulb was old; it shone a dim yellow and was barely effective. Daniel wondered if the light bulbs had all been in the house when Cho had had the electricity turned back on, and whether she had thought about replacing them or whether new light would upset some feng shui balance. He supposed it would be up to him if he wanted better lighting after dark.

He sauntered down to the pink corner room, where the wall had been removed on the hallway side. He paused, taking a sip of his beer and another bite of his sandwich. He had managed to remove half of the wall. He had stopped at the pink door when he realized it was load-bearing; after that, he had stripped it down to the bare frame until he could get the proper structural support in place.

He took another sip and gazed through the open wall into the pink bedroom. Even in the evening, it didn't seem so tomb-like now that one of the walls had been removed.

The staccato night sounds from the bayou filtered in from

outside; he looked over at the dirty window and saw a swirl of flickering fireflies far below in the front yard.

A cell phone echoed from the distance in the old house. Daniel hesitated, checked his pockets. Shit. His phone was downstairs. He set his beer on the cross brace in the open wall and hurried away.

Daniel snapped on another overhead light at the foot of the stairs in the living room; the phone rang again. He saw it on top of his toolbox by the coffee table, hurried over and grabbed it.

"It's Daniel," he grunted, as he cleared his throat.

"Daniel, It's Eileen Cho." The older woman's voice crackled distantly over the line.

"Oh, hey. How's it goin'?"

There was a moment of silence before she continued, "Is everything all right there?"

"Here? Everything's goin' great. We actually got pretty far today. Most of the small bedroom wall upstairs and all of the living..."

"No," she cut him off. "I mean with you."

Daniel hesitated a moment, sensing the tension in her voice. "What do you mean?"

"I'm not sure, exactly. I just wanted to make sure you..." Her voice dropped away.

"Hello?" Daniel moved toward the window, trying to get a better signal. "Hello?"

Cho's voice popped back in. "...got a feeling...been bothering me..." Then she dropped out again.

"Shit," Daniel muttered, annoyed. He moved along the wall to the door.

Cho's voice crackled back in again. "...maybe nothing, but I just wanted to call and make sure. Are you there, Daniel?"

"Yeah, I'm here. But you're cutting out pretty bad. Eileen?"

"Daniel?"

"Yeah. Look, Eileen. Everything's fine. Don't worry about me, all right?" Daniel waited a moment for her to reply. There was nothing. "Hello? You still there?"

Daniel pressed the phone tighter to his ear, and after a moment, he could hear Cho's faint voice. "Just be careful, Daniel."

"I will. I mean, I'm fine—" BEEP. BEEP. BEEP. The line went completely dead. "Hello?" Daniel said one last time, but he knew it was pointless. He lowered the phone and punched it off. "What the hell was that about?" he muttered to himself.

Daniel remained for a moment in the dark living room; the dim yellow overhead bulb was no match now for the darkness that had enveloped the old house. It cast a hazy maze of shadows through the construction mess and the furniture crowded in the center of the room. The sounds of the shrill crickets and burping frogs outside were more defined than the wash of cicada noise during the day. A hollow cry from a bird or an owl echoed from somewhere in the distance. The plastic tarp over the open entryway rattled as it swayed gently in a slight breeze. No doubt about it, this place was eerie at night.

Daniel set his phone back onto his toolbox and crossed to the kitchen. He kneeled down and opened the cooler. He dredged his hand through the ice, feeling for a beer. Nothing except for a couple of tightly wrapped sandwiches. No beer.

"Damn." He slammed the lid, wiped his cold hand on his pants, and looked over at a pile of beer cans on the kitchen floor nearby. Had he really gone through twelve beers this afternoon? "Sure don't last like they used to," he mumbled, as if someone were there to hear him.

He stood, feeling the disappointment set in. He was just about to let it go when he remembered he had left a beer upstairs. He had barely taken a couple of drinks from it when the cell rang, and he had set it on the cross brace in the open wall. Perfect.

Daniel climbed the stairs two steps at a time, reached the

upstairs hall, and paused, catching his breath. The overhead light bulb here was also barely doing its job against the darkness. He crossed down the hallway, already tasting the cold brew streaming down his sticky, hot throat, and reached the open wall at the corner room-

The beer was gone.

Daniel scanned the entire open frame. All of the cross braces were empty. Nothing there. No can of beer.

"Gimme a break," Daniel groaned. He looked down at the rubble beneath the open wall. Nothing. Was he losing his fucking mind? Did he put it down somewhere else? No, he didn't. He was sure he put it right here. Didn't he? First the hammer, and now this.

"This is fucking nuts!" he barked angrily. His voice echoed throughout the large house. He rubbed his eyes tiredly and tried to focus his mind more clearly. He had to re-trace what he had done. First, he came inside after Reggie left, then he went to the kitchen. He got the beer and the sandwich. Then he went upstairs. He definitely had the beer in his hand when he came upstairs, and....

A woman's faint scream drifted to him from the distance.

Daniel mind snapped back to the present. He waited in silence, holding his breath, listening. After a moment, he heard it again, louder this time, and closer. There was no mistaking what it was: A blood-curdling, desperate scream, coming from outside the house.

Daniel rushed to the window of the pink bedroom and looked out. Through the dingy glass, he saw a barefoot teenage girl in cut-offs staggering up the driveway; her torn blouse and bare legs were splattered with blood.

She clutched the oozing wound in her neck where the knife blade had grazed her in the boathouse.

FIVE

"Jesus fucking Christ." Daniel grabbed the window jamb and yanked hard. It was painted shut. He yelled futilely, "Hey!" His voice rang in his ears.

The girl outside in the driveway hobbled anxiously closer to the house, then she stopped and looked back into the misty bayou behind her. There was panic and terror in her eyes. She shot another look at the house, then over at the old barn. The barn was much closer. She cut toward it.

Daniel watched her as she disappeared into the dilapidated old structure. "Shit!" He spun from the window, clambered across the pile of boxes in the center of the room, and ran out into the hall.

He bounded down the steps three at a time and careened into the living room, slamming his shin hard on the coffee table. "Fuck!"

But the sharp pain wasn't enough to slow him down. He burst through the plastic sheeting in the entryway and threw open the front door.

"Hey!" Daniel yelled as he leaped off the porch and ran down the walkway. He paused at the gate, squinting into the misty darkness where he had seen the girl. If anyone was chasing her, Daniel couldn't see who it was. He pushed through the gate and ran to the barn, pausing in the entrance to catch his breath. He scanned the shadowy, cavernous space. Pale moonlight filtered through the slats in the rotting wood walls.

"Hello?" No reply. He stepped inside, clearing a dusty cobweb out of his way as he went. A metallic CLANK came from the shadows beyond a stack of molding hay bales.

Daniel hesitated; he could hear his heart pounding in his ears and feel his lungs aching after his short but reckless sprint from the house. He started in the direction the sound had come from. As he pushed past the rotting stack of hay bales, a collection of rusting farm tools leaning against an old tractor came into view.

Daniel paused, squinting into the shadowy maze in front of him. He had definitely seen her enter the barn. He was sure of that. So where was she?

Daniel exhaled audibly, and he was about to take another step when a pitchfork rose up out of the darkness behind him. He stopped cold, sensing the threatening presence, then spun around just as the pitchfork stabbed viciously downward. Daniel dived out of the way at the last second; the sharp talons of the pitchfork sank into the soft dirt floor. He regained his footing, looked up, and saw the girl, about eighteen, he guessed, brandishing the pitchfork.

The terrified girl stared at him for a brief moment. Then she dropped the pitchfork and staggered toward him, breathing, "Help...help me." She collapsed into Daniel's arms.

"What happened to you?"

She looked up at him, swallowing hard, out of breath; blood was splattered on her girlish but beautiful face. "He...he's coming," she gasped.

"What? Who? Who's coming?" Daniel stammered. "The guy

who did this to you?" He tried to make sense out of the bizarre situation.

The girl coughed, trying to get more words out, but it was too painful. Daniel squinted at the deep, bloody knife wound above her collarbone. Any higher and it would have hit her carotid artery and she would have bled to death. He shifted her in his arms, taking more of her weight. "It's all right. Don't try to talk," he said. "I'll take care of it. Come on, I've got a phone in the house."

Daniel helped her several steps toward the door, and her legs gave out. "Okay. I've got you." He scooped her legs up and carried her out of the barn. She was lighter than he thought she'd be, probably just over a hundred pounds; her body was gracefully toned and lean, her legs long.

He glanced back down the driveway into the misty darkness as he crossed to the porch. Still no sign of whoever was chasing her. He struggled with the screen door latch and managed to pull it open.

He pushed through the plastic sheeting and into the living room, where he tossed off the dust cover and laid her on the couch, which had been pushed against the other furniture so that its cushions faced outward. "Keep putting pressure on your neck," he said. "I just have to get my phone."

She nodded, frightened. Daniel hurried back to the center of the room where the furniture had been stacked and stopped dead in his tracks.

His toolbox and his phone were both gone.

"Son of a..." He spun around, frantically scanning the dark room. "Where the hell?"

The girl shifted on the couch and gasped in pain. Daniel's attention returned to her. "Keep the pressure on," he said. He made a quick search around the stacked furniture. She moaned again.

"Fuck it. We'll drive out of here!" Daniel raced across the dark kitchen to the small maid's quarters, where he had stashed his duffle and belongings. The small room was pitch black. He fumbled around for a light switch, found it, and snapped it on.

His duffle bag and belongings were also gone.

Daniel stared at the empty bed for a moment, stunned. "What the fuck is going on?"

The girl's scream echoed from somewhere deep in the house. Daniel turned and bolted out through the kitchen. He raced into the living room.

The girl wasn't there.

"Jesus Christ," he said.

The girl's scream came again, from upstairs. Daniel raced to the stairwell and flew up the steps to the hallway. There was another blood-curdling scream from the pink room at the far end of the dark hall. He raced down to the open wall and skidded to a stop in the rubble.

There was no one in the pink room.

Daniel spun back. Maybe he had heard it wrong. "Where are you?" he screamed desperately. There was no answer. He ran to the master bedroom. It, too, was empty.

Daniel tore at his hair, exasperated. "Where the fuck?" He bounded back downstairs to the living room, panting heavily, adrenaline surging. "Where did you go?" he yelled. But there was no answer. The house was silent.

He paced back into the center of the room, lost and frantic. Then he saw them.

His toolbox and cell phone were back on the coffee table.

Daniel stopped breathing. His eyes locked on his returned belongings. What the hell was happening?

He crossed back to the kitchen and went into the small maid's room.

His duffle bag and clothes were on the small bed, just the way they were supposed to be. And the girl had vanished.

SIX

It took a little over an hour before the Krotz Springs police cruiser showed up at the house. It was a fancy, late-model Ford with all the trimmings. For a small town, they took their law enforcement seriously, Daniel thought, as he watched it pull to a stop.

As Daniel stood across from the heavyset deputy in a tan sweat-stained shirt, he was sure they must have saved a bundle on deputy salaries. The guy must be in his '60s, and he looked like someone who had answered a casting notice for a backwoods Cajun deputy. Daniel couldn't help but think about all those old Burt Reynolds movies he used to watch on TV when he was a kid. It would have been funny if the situation hadn't been so serious.

"So this was the last place you saw her?" the deputy asked as he stabbed his thick finger at the couch.

"That's right. I left her here so I could get my truck keys."

The fat man peered through his bifocals at the notes he was jotting down. "Then you heard her scream."

"Yeah, and I came out, but she was gone." Daniel watched a bead of sweat roll slowly down a crease in the jiggling folds of the deputy's neck as he wrote Daniel's words on his notepad. The old guy didn't understand this. Not really. Maybe Daniel wasn't making it clear enough. "Her scream," he tried to explain. "It...it wasn't like anything I'd heard before. It was horrible, like she was being hurt."

The deputy peered back up at Daniel. "Coming from the pink corner room upstairs, where we looked?"

"That's what I thought, but with all these open walls and stuff, everything kinda echoes. It had to have been outside. Whoever was after her must have pulled her back outside."

The deputy's droopy face stared blankly at him. Daniel could almost see the wheels in his thick head trying to turn and make sense of this. The deputy sniffed, looked back down at his notes, and wrote some more.

Daniel sighed. This was getting to be downright annoying. How stupid could this fat fuck be?

"Look, I know this all seems a little weird, but..."

"Does it?" The old guy looked back up over his bifocals.

"Well, I mean...just the fact that I don't know where she could have gone and all...and my phone..."

"What about your phone?"

"I...I couldn't find it when I needed it, and..." Daniel stammered.

The deputy waited for Daniel to continue. Daniel realized he could blow his credibility if he started going into a story about all his vanishing and re-appearing belongings. He decided he had to skip it. "But I did find it. That's how I called you."

The deputy looked at Daniel for another moment, his watery blue eyes studying him. His sweaty face didn't seem so stupid now. "You never got her name?"

"No, I was just focused on trying to help her." Daniel couldn't help but think he was the one sounding stupid now, so he added, "Look, she's got to be out there someplace. She's probably hurt.

He might have taken her someplace. We should get some people in here and start trying to find her."

The deputy was staring blankly again at Daniel. But now, Daniel realized it wasn't a blank stare; it was a poker face. There was plenty going on inside the old fat man's head, plenty of years of law enforcement and character reading.

"You come over from Huston?"

"Yeah, got here this morning."

The deputy looked over at the pile of beer cans on the floor of the kitchen by the cooler. "All that stuff's yours?"

Shit. Daniel could see where this was going, and he knew he had to shut it down as fast as he could. "Officer, I only had a few beers. I'm sober, trust me."

"Those are from the whole day, then?"

"Yeah. Look, this really happened. I'm sure of it. I saw it...I saw her. She was in my arms. I helped her inside."

"You change?"

"What?" Daniel asked, thrown by the non sequitur.

"Your shirt."

"What about it?"

"You changed your shirt." Now it was the deputy who was getting annoyed. "You said this girl was covered with blood."

Daniel looked down at his dirty T-shirt.

There were no bloodstains.

"You said you carried her into the house from the barn. You said she was bleeding pretty heavy."

Game over.

Daniel was out and he knew it. He could avoid mentioning his missing phone and belongings, but he couldn't hide from this. There was no blood on his shirt. There was no blood on the cushions of the couch, or on the floor. There was no blood anywhere.

After a moment, Daniel could only stammer out a reply. "It...

it was mainly on her neck and face…" He trailed off, realizing how pathetic his attempt to explain sounded.

The deputy closed his notebook. He sucked his thick upper lip for a second, deliberating, then said, "Krotz Springs is a small town. If she's anyone from around here, we're gonna know it pretty quick. I'll do some callin' around." The deputy slid his notebook into his back pocket and started to the front door.

Daniel watched the older man walking away. This wasn't ending the way it should; there was a girl out there bleeding and in danger. Daniel couldn't help himself. "That's it?"

The deputy hesitated at the front door, then turned back to look at Daniel with that poker face. "Well, I don't have a body. I don't have any physical evidence of a crime. All I've got is a possible missing person…"

"Who could be bleeding to death out there!" Daniel finished his sentence angrily.

For the first time, the fat old face registered a reaction. And it wasn't good. His watery eyes narrowed slightly, and he continued in a low, even voice, "You know what else I've got? I've got a man who's most rightly chockay from drinking all day, who can't tell where sounds are coming from, and who sees vanishing people." There was a moment of silence for emphasis before the deputy continued pointedly, "But then that would be a whole different report, and that's a report that would probably end up with someone spending the night in the drunk tank."

The message couldn't be any clearer. Daniel eased back silently. The deputy turned back to the door. "I've got your number, Mr. Nash. I might be callin'." Then, the old guy couldn't help himself. A sarcastic smile flickered on his big lips. "Just try not to lose your phone again, huh?" He pushed out the screen door and was gone.

Daniel took a few steps to the door and looked outside. He watched the deputy ease his big frame into the squad car.

"Asshole," Daniel muttered to himself. The deputy fired up the cruiser and roared off down the driveway.

————

Reggie arrived promptly at 6:45 the next morning. He parked his pick-up by the front gate, grabbed a bag of groceries and his tool belt from the truck bed, and started to the house. When he reached the gate, he saw Daniel sitting on the porch steps in the shadows.

"Oh, hey. I brought more beer. And I got you the groceries you asked for." As Reggie grew closer, he could see Daniel more clearly. He was still wearing the same dirty work clothes, and the expression of someone who hadn't slept all night. "Dude, you better get some coffee into your sorry ass," Reggie said. "You look like shit."

Daniel rose from the steps and took the groceries from Reggie. "Thanks." He started into the house. "Leave your tool belt here. We're leavin'."

"Leavin'? Where we going?"

"Back behind the house to start, then down along the river," Daniel answered from inside the open door.

"What the hell is going on?"

Twenty minutes later, Daniel was leading the way through the thick brush behind the house. The air was already hot and sticky, and the cicadas added to the oppressive feeling with their unending thrum.

"And she didn't say who was after her? No name, or nothing like that?" Reggie asked.

"Nothing. She said 'he' was coming. That's it. 'He.'"

Reggie ran the story that Daniel had told him over in his head for a moment, and he snorted incredulously. "Dude, that is some weird shit."

"Yeah. Tell me about it."

"Of course, it don't surprise me that fat ass Officer Clemmens wasn't no help. That lazy ol' fuck won't even lift his prick to piss."

"Yeah well, lazy or not, he was pretty sure I was out of my mind by the time he left here." Daniel slowed his pace, squinting in the hot morning sunlight. He saw the isolated road up ahead. "River's on the other side of the road?"

"Yeah. North end of the Atchafalaya," Reggie answered, and followed Daniel as he pushed his way through the rest of the brush to the road embankment. Daniel scrambled up first and held out his hand for Reggie.

Reggie just laughed at the hand. "I been bouncing around in these woods my whole life. Don't need your help."

He climbed up the embankment and joined Daniel on the road. They paused a moment, catching their breath. There was a Ford Fiesta parked off on the shoulder a few yards down the road.

Daniel shot a look at Reggie. "Nothing around here for miles, right?"

"Nothin' but your house and the swamp," Reggie confirmed.

Daniel pulled a branch out of the bramble on the side of the road. He swung it a few times, testing its strength, then started toward the car. Reggie followed "You gonna switch somebody with that?"

Daniel shot him a look. "Shhhh," he hissed.

They stepped quietly up to the car and Daniel peered through the dirty side window. There was no one inside. He dropped the stick, cupped his hand to shield the glare, and leaned toward the glass. There was a pink Krotz Springs High School binder on the passenger seat and a pair of women's boots on the floor beneath. There was a make-up compact in the ashtray. "Looks like it belongs to a high school girl," he said.

He looked into the back window. There were several other schoolbooks scattered on the back seat and a rumpled blouse.

Daniel rose and scanned the surrounding bayou with a troubled look on his face. Reggie tried the door handle. It was locked. He reached for the back door.

"Don't. Don't touch it."

"Why not?"

"Just...you don't know. Might have to get prints off the handles."

"You think this belongs to the girl you saw last night?"

"Could be. Maybe." Daniel went around to the hood and placed his hand on it. It was warm.

"What're you thinkin'?"

"Not sure. Could be warm from the morning sun, or it could've been running recently." Daniel looked across the far side of the road at the river. "Come on." He started down the embankment. Reggie followed.

The brush was thicker here and the ground was soggy. They emerged onto the edge of the river. A path led along the bank of the slow-moving black water. Daniel looked across the deep, watery expanse. "Doubt she'd make it across that," he said.

"Yeah, probably right," Reggie agreed.

Daniel looked up the path. "I'll go up here a piece. How about you head down the other way?"

"It's your dime, boss. You want me to swing a hammer or do this, it's all the same to me." Reggie looked down at the stick that Daniel was carrying, then reached over to the edge of the path and pulled a thicker one out of the brush. "I don't know what you're expectin' to find, but I sure as shit ain't gonna be caught short," he said.

Daniel smiled and started up the path. Reggie went the other way.

The path along the river was muddy and worn with footprints. Probably from the kids that came out this way to party, Daniel thought. He tried to see if he could tell if any were fresh, but the mud made it impossible. He looked up from the prints and scanned the surrounding bayou for any sign of the girl. The air was still and hot. There was no sign of anyone.

He pushed his way through a partially overgrown stretch in the path and paused, wiping the sweat off his brow. He looked up at the sun, peering through the long strands of moss hanging eerily over him. A dragonfly flitted past. The hot, insistent sound of cicadas rose in the distance.

Daniel looked back down at the path in front of him and was about to start forward when he heard a faint, desperate cry.

Daniel stopped cold and listened. After a moment, he heard it again. It was somewhere up the path. It was a woman's cry.

Daniel sprung into action. He rushed down the path, rounded a bend and saw a dilapidated boathouse on the riverbank several yards ahead. He skidded to a stop and listened again. The woman's gasp came from the boathouse. She was obviously struggling with someone inside.

Daniel's heart began to race. He took a shallow breath and crept quietly over to the shack. He stepped out onto the creaking wood deck. The sounds of struggle were louder. He could see shadowy, violent movement through the rotting slats of wood. The woman gasped and cried out sharply.

Daniel's palms were damp as he gripped the stick tightly and approached the door. He took a deep breath, reared back, and gave it a mighty kick.

Two high-school teens were up against the far wall, their naked bodies slamming feverishly against each other in a rutting frenzy.

The girl saw Daniel first and screamed. She shoved her boyfriend aside. The young man spun around awkwardly, his erection bobbing and wagging comically. "What the fuck?" he gasped between heavy breaths.

Daniel quickly raised his hands in an attempt to show he meant no harm. "I...I thought someone was hurt here... I..."

The moment grew more awkward until Daniel backed out the door, as the mortified girl tugged the bottom of her tank top down below her waist and gathered her skirt and panties off the floor.

"I'm sorry," Daniel muttered sheepishly as he closed the door.

———

Reggie's laughter rolled out across the bayou. "You sure taught those poor little bastards not to stop off for a quickie before school again, you can bet your ass on that." He almost collapsed into laughter as he followed Daniel up the driveway to the house.

It took Daniel a good twenty minutes before he could see the humor in the whole situation, and even then, he could only smile and nod. But it was pure comic gold for Reggie. "That poor girl's gonna think twice next time she decides to do the nasty," he cackled as they approached the porch.

"What do you say we get some work done, huh?" Daniel smiled as he grabbed his tool belt.

"Hey, I'm on it. Wasn't my idea to go wandering off into the swamp." Reggie chuckled again to himself as he climbed the steps and entered the house.

Daniel strapped on his belt and paused for a moment. He looked back down the driveway at the surrounding bayou. The smile faded on his face. The Ford Fiesta with the high school girl's possessions in it probably belonged to the couple in the boathouse, not to someone wandering the woods in pain. But no matter what had happened this morning, it didn't change what had happened last night. Whoever the girl was, she could still be out there.

He turned and climbed the steps.

SEVEN

REGGIE STAYED after work that night. This time, he had a single beer with Daniel, then he left, promising to be in Monday morning at the usual time. Daniel hadn't realized it was Saturday night. Things like that didn't seem important anymore. During Angie's long decline and death, he had grown used to letting the days run from one to the next with no distinction. He had perfected the art of killing time.

It was Saturday night, and the only difference it made was that Reggie wouldn't be there the next day. So what? He could still work if he wanted to. It would give him something to do.

Daniel sat alone in the living room on the couch, which Reggie had shrouded again against construction dust. He sipped the latest in a succession of beers that must have totaled an even dozen by this point. The overhead bulb glowed dimly, casting eerie shadows through the partially demolished room. He thought again about the girl he hadn't been able to help the night before, and a feeling he hadn't felt in a long time began to creep up on him. It was a nauseous feeling in the pit of his stomach. It was the same feeling he had felt every time Angie's cancer had failed to respond to the latest treatment.

Daniel drained his can of beer and tossed it aside. It hit the hardwood floor with a hollow bang and rattled into a dark corner. Fuck it. He wasn't going to go there. He wasn't going to let himself be swallowed up again by the black abyss. There had to be something he could do. There was a mystery here and he needed to solve it.

He reached into his pocket and took out his cell phone. It had disappeared while she was in the house, and it had reappeared when she was gone. The same with the toolboxes and his belongings. But why? Were they somehow connected? Had the girl been outside when his hammer had disappeared and reappeared? Did her presence cause the things to disappear? How? And why?

Daniel set his cell phone on the toolbox where it had been the night before, then eased back on the couch. He stared at the phone for a moment, then got up and grabbed another beer from the cooler and headed upstairs.

He cracked open the new beer and took a long drink as he strolled down the cluttered hall. When he reached the open wall to the pink room, he stopped. He took another long swig, then set the beer on the cross brace.

He stood for a moment in the silence, then crossed the pink room to the window. It was a muggy night. Just like last night. Same night sounds, same encroaching swamp.

He waited. The moment passed uneventfully. He waited longer. He was determined to find out what had happened to the girl, and to do that, he felt he had to recreate the events that had happened the night before. But what made him think there was even a remote possibility of doing that? He didn't have an answer. Just a feeling that he should try. But it was a strong feeling.

Another quiet moment passed, and he shifted his gaze to his reflection in the dirty glass. His two-day growth had stretched into four and was visible even in the dark reflection. He had really let himself go. He needed to take a shower and have a good shave. But somehow, it didn't seem so important now. Somehow the only thing that seemed important now was....

What the fuck was he doing? Daniel became aware of how absurd his thinking was. Try to recreate last night? This is how it starts when people lose it, he thought. They think something is rational when it's completely absurd. He was losing his grip. And there was no one there to grab on to.

He turned away from the window and went out of the room. He grabbed the beer off the cross brace and took another long swig as he trudged downstairs. Jesus Christ. What the hell made him even start thinking like this?

He paused at the foot of the stairs and snapped off the overhead light, then crossed to the kitchen. He drained the beer, tossed the can into the pile by the cooler and entered his little room.

It was hot and stuffy in the small quarters. He left the door open and plopped onto the bed. Shit. Had his depression gotten so bad he was losing control? Maybe he needed to see a professional. A doctor. A psychologist. Someone. Daniel considered his options: Krotz Springs was such an out-of-the-way little town there was no way he'd be able to find a qualified doctor for something like this. He'd have to go to New Orleans. First, he'd have to find one, then make an appointment. It would mean he'd probably have to take a day off from the remodel to do it. But what choice did he have? Ignore this? He couldn't. Not the way he was starting to feel.

It was settled, then. Tomorrow he'd look into it. He'd try to find a recommendation from....

The little bed was empty.

What?

The bed. It was empty.

Daniel looked down the length of the bed and over to the old chair by the bathroom door. No duffle bag. No belongings. None of his stuff was there. It was gone.

It was happening again.

Daniel shot to his feet and hurried into the living room, fumbling for the light switch by the kitchen as he went. He managed to snap it on, and the dim yellow light illuminated the living room.

His toolboxes and cell phone were gone again.

Yes. It was happening. Daniel's mouth went dry. His heart started racing. He hurried over to the coffee table to make sure he wasn't mistaken. He wasn't. His cell phone and toolbox were gone.

A bloodcurdling scream shattered the silence. Daniel raced to the front window and peered out.

The same girl emerged from the darkness down the driveway, running toward the house. She was covered with blood and clutching her wounded neck, just like before.

"Jesus Christ." Daniel shoved his way through the plastic sheeting in the entrance way, raced to the front door, and threw it open. "Hey!" he yelled.

This time the girl stopped in the driveway, startled.

Daniel hurried out onto the front porch. The girl staggered back away from him and shot a panicked look behind her. A confused, trapped look flooded her face.

"No, no. It's okay. I'm not going to hurt you, remember?" Daniel said as he approached her cautiously.

She shot another look behind her at the dark bayou. Daniel stopped advancing and reached out sympathetically. "It's gonna be all right. I won't leave you alone this time, I promise."

His reassuring words did nothing to ease the confused look on her face. "Wh... who... are you?"

"Daniel. Daniel Nash," he answered, as if that would mean something to her.

She grimaced in pain, clutching her neck wound. Her legs turned rubbery beneath her. Daniel stepped up and caught her. "Come on, let's get inside."

Daniel helped her toward the house. She looked up at him, frightened, but the pain she was in left her no choice but to accept help from this stranger.

"I looked all over the place for you today. By the river, along the road. Everywhere."

"For me?" she gasped, looking at him strangely, still fighting the pain.

"Of course. After you disappeared last night, I've been going crazy trying to find you."

"I don't know what you're talking about."

Daniel looked down at her bewildered expression. "Last night. You don't remember?"

She shook her head slightly, growing wary of the strange man who was being so helpful.

Daniel took a moment to consider what this could mean. It didn't make sense that she wouldn't remember, but he didn't want to spook her any more, so he decided to leave it alone for now, "What's your name?"

"Cl... Claire...," she whispered.

"Claire?"

She nodded, then added "Wayn... Waynright."

Daniel helped her up the steps and onto the porch. The extra effort was painful and she staggered, "It's okay. Easy. Take it easy."

Daniel shoved open the screen door and pushed the plastic sheeting aside. She looked at the strange surroundings as if she were in a foreign land. Daniel closed the door behind them and locked the deadbolt.

"Over to the couch," he said as he steered her into the dark room, then detoured to the kitchen, grabbed a dish towel from a drawer, and hurried back to her, again flinging the dust cover from the couch.

Renewed panic filled Claire's eyes "Please... don't let him get me. He's trying to kill me."

Daniel helped her down onto the couch and gently took her hand. "Look, I don't know what this is all about, but you can count on me. I won't let him get you." Daniel looked deep into her uncertain, terrified eyes, "Really," he said. "You can trust me. I promise. Okay?"

After a few seconds, Claire nodded and let go of his hand. "Okay."

"Good. Good. Now here. Keep this on your neck." Daniel handed her the dishtowel, and she pressed it to the oozing knife wound above her collarbone.

He gave her a reassuring smile, then got up and looked around the room. He needed something to defend himself. Something heavy. Something lethal. He spotted a kindling hatchet by the fireplace, and he hurried over and grabbed it. It was small and heavy and could definitely do some damage if he needed it to.

He crossed back to the front window, pulled the curtain aside and peered out. "Who is he? Who's after you?"

Claire took a shaky breath, "I...I don't know him."

There was movement in the misty darkness down the driveway. Daniel wiped the dirty windowpane and adjusted his angle. A shadowy figure emerged, walking at a menacing, steady pace toward them.

"Does he have a gun? Anything like that?"

"A knife. He has a knife."

Daniel looked back at Claire; one hand clutched her torn blouse tightly, holding it closed, and the other hand pressed the towel to her wound. The bare overhead bulb bathed her in dim yellow light. Shit. The man could see them from out there with the light on.

Daniel hurried over to the switch at the foot of the stairs and snapped it off. The pale blue light filtered in from the windows; now, it was reversed. They could see him and he couldn't see them.

Daniel made his way back to the window, pressed into the shadows against the wall, and pulled the curtain aside. The menacing figure grew closer, emerging from the dark mist. He was tall, and he appeared to be in his early 20s. He wore a blood-splattered T-shirt and carried a large hunting knife, but Daniel couldn't make out his face in the darkness.

As the killer reached the gate in the front yard, Daniel ducked back from the window. He heard the heavy footsteps climb the front porch steps and cross to the door. Daniel pressed back into the shadows next to the door and raised the hatchet. The footsteps stopped. The man was right there, just on the other side of the door. Daniel could feel his presence. There was a low creak as the killer shifted his weight.

Daniel looked down at the doorknob. It clicked clockwise then stopped and turned in the other direction. There was a pause, and the door creaked in its frame as the killer leaned against it on the other side.

Daniel tightened his grip on the hatchet and stopped breathing. The moment seemed like an eternity, then the door creaked again as the killer eased his weight from the other side of it. Daniel exhaled.

The heavy footsteps thumped away down the porch; Daniel followed their direction with his eyes as the sounds moved to the kitchen window. He looked over at Claire, raised his finger to his lips signaling her to be quiet, and crept over to the kitchen. The killer's shadow passed outside the window, heading for the back door. Shit. Was it locked?

Daniel ran through the kitchen, slamming his hip against the counter in the darkness. He grimaced, holding back any sound, and stumbled to the back door. He grabbed the lock and gave it a twist. It was secure.

Daniel slid up against the wall beside the door as he had in the living room. His heart thundered in his chest, his hip throbbed in pain. He could feel the beads of sweat trickling down his forehead, but he didn't make a move to wipe them away. He kept his eyes locked on the door and the hatchet poised to strike at the first sign of any breach.

"Daniel," Claire's soft voice shattered the silence. Daniel looked over and saw her silhouetted across the kitchen on the other side of the open wall. "Daniel, I'm scared."

"Shhhh," he admonished her gently; the last thing Daniel wanted now was for the killer to hear her.

She hesitated, then lowered her voice to a whisper. "I don't want to be alone."

"It's okay," he whispered. "Go back into the living room. Keep quiet."

She hesitated, reluctant to leave his sight. A low creak came from the back steps. Daniel looked at the door, then back to Claire. He nodded to the door and mouthed the words, "He's right there."

Renewed fear filled Claire's eyes; she silently slipped back into the living room, out of sight.

Daniel returned his attention to the back door. He shifted his grip on the hatchet and waited. A moment passed, then another.

There were no more sounds outside.

No more creaks on the steps. No attempt to try this door. No sound of him retreating. Nothing. Just the hypnotic, staccato night sounds of the bayou outside.

Was it possible the killer had given up and left? Maybe he hadn't seen Claire enter the house, and he had gone off to check the barn.

Daniel took his eyes off the back door. He turned and scanned the shadowy kitchen. How long was he going to stay here? What else could he do? He turned to leave the kitchen.

Claire's blood-curdling scream shattered the stillness.

Adrenaline shocked Daniel to the core; he bolted across the dark kitchen and spun into the living room. "Claire?"

He scanned the dark maze of shadows. The couch was empty. No sign of Claire.

"Claire!"

The plastic sheeting rattled from a muggy breeze that swirled through the room. Daniel reeled around and saw the curtain blowing in an open side window. "God, no," he whispered. The window hadn't been open before. The killer had gotten inside.

Claire's scream echoed again through the dark house. A low thump resonated from the ceiling.

She was upstairs.

Daniel raced to the staircase and bounded up the steps. He tore down the hallway to the pink room at the far end and skidded to a stop in the rubble by the open wall. Claire's scream shot out of the room. For a brief moment, Daniel saw a blur of violent movement in the shadowy far corner. A knife blade glinted in the moonlight as it slashed downward.

"Claire!"

Daniel burst across the room and to the corner.

It was empty.

EIGHT

Daniel spun around, frantically scanning the construction rubble and the dusty furniture. There was no one there.

No. How could it be? She was just here. He heard her. He saw her.

He looked back at the empty corner. Wait. What exactly *had* he seen?

Daniel started sinking again.

He could feel his stomach knot and a wave of nausea sweep over him. The room around him felt distant. He staggered out into the hallway and leaned against the wall to steady himself. His breathing was shallow, and his legs were starting to go numb. Maybe he was mistaken. Maybe what he had seen were shadows from the trees outside, making patterns on the floor. Claire could still be downstairs someplace. He pushed himself down the hall to the stairs and descended into the living room. He snapped on the light and froze.

His toolboxes were back by the coffee table. His cell phone was on top, where he had put it.

Daniel stumbled over, grabbed his phone. Yes. It was real. He kicked the toolboxes. Solid.

Daniel spun around, yelling desperately. "What the fuck is going on?" His voice echoed away into nothingness.

Daniel collapsed onto the couch and closed his eyes; he tried to steady himself. It had happened just the way it had before: When Claire was there, his things were missing. When she disappeared, his things came back. Was she real? Were his things real? Was this house real? Claire. Waynright. Her name. The name of the house. She was connected with it. Who was she? The owner of the pink room? Was that why she came here after she was attacked? Was she running home?

The only thing that seemed certain was that something horrible had happened to Claire both times he had seen her. He tried to play back in his head the brief flashes of what he had witnessed upstairs. The images were dark and disorienting, but he was certain he had seen a knife, and he was certain he had heard Claire scream.

He opened his eyes, and the dark, sinking feeling of guilt and helplessness returned.

He had failed.

He had failed Angie. And now he had failed Claire. Not once. Twice.

A shaky whisper escaped Daniel. "What the fuck is happening to me?"

———

Daniel stared numbly at the pale morning light that began to glow through the dirty windows. He hadn't moved from the couch all night. His body was frozen, but his mind was racing. He had retraced every moment over and over, trying to make sense of what had happened. Any rational explanations didn't fit. So that left only irrational explanations. Paranormal explanations. Ghosts.

At a different time in his life, Daniel would have dismissed these ideas. He would have considered them insane, or at the least fanciful, wishful thinking.

But not now. During Angie's slow decline, he had thought long and hard about things he couldn't touch, smell, or see. He had spent countless sleepless nights anguishing over the "what ifs" of death. Was he going to lose Angie to nothingness? Was the end of life like a computer that just shuts off? Or was there something else? Did we move on or stay in this realm in a different form? Heaven? Hell? Were they myths and legends? The endless agonizing over Angie's fate went on for months. There seemed to be no end to the spiraling thoughts and no answers to satisfy him.

Ultimately, time became his salvation. The more days he endured, the less painful the questions became, and in the end, the questions he had tortured himself with had faded away unanswered.

But now they were back with a vengeance. The feeling in Daniel's gut was driving him now. Even if he didn't know what questions to ask regarding Claire's mysterious appearances, it seemed certain that she did belong to the pink room upstairs, and that the answers had to be in that room.

Daniel checked his watch: It was closing in on 7 a.m., Sunday morning. Daniel would be alone all day and night today. He rose from the couch, crossed the room, and climbed the stairs.

The upstairs hall was dingy in the morning light; a coating of construction dust covered everything. He continued down the hall to the pink bedroom and stepped through the open wall. He paused for a moment, taking in the surroundings. Whatever had been precious and orderly in the girl's room had been violated by the construction. The furniture and storage boxes were now piled in the center under a tarp. It was hard to remember what it had looked like when he had first opened the door.

Daniel pulled back the tarp. He coughed from the construction dust that billowed up; he grabbed a screwdriver off the ladder and dug into one of the sealed boxes, ripping off the lid. It was filled with stuffed animals.

He opened the next box. There were old textbooks and Krotz Springs High School binders. He shoved the box aside and opened a third.

This was more like it. Personal keepsakes. Horse show ribbons, school yearbooks, a graduation tassel. He pulled out a handful of horse show ribbons and stopped cold. There was a 7th grade school picture staring up at him from beneath them.

He pulled the photo out of the box and gazed at the young girl's face: Mousy brown hair, blue eyes, and a tentative smile that barely hid her braces.

It was definitely Claire. Much younger, but definitely Claire. He was right. She had been running to safety, running home.

Daniel set the photo aside and looked back into the box. There was a small pink book with a brass clasp holding it closed. A diary.

Daniel pulled it out, unsnapped the latch, and opened it. The handwriting was round and neat. Each word seemed to have been carefully weighed and considered. *"I hate my braces. The more Mom tells me I have a pretty smile, the less I want to smile. I don't have a pretty smile. I have braces and they are ugly. Maybe I am too. No boys look at me the way they look at Tina Harding. I know what they see. I'm not stupid."*

The entry ended. Daniel flipped through the book. The entries became shorter and more sporadic. He stopped when he found a longer one. Years later. She was a high school freshman.

"Sadie Hawkins Day. The most sadistic, cruel concept that anyone could come up with. Roger Franks didn't say anything for at least two minutes after I asked him to the dance. Do you know how long two minutes is? It's insanely long. I wanted to crawl away and die right there. By the time he mumbled something that I can't even remember, I was so mortified I couldn't even look at

him. Nothing is going right for me this year. I don't belong here. I don't belong anywhere."

Roger slowly leaned back and closed the book. He sat for a moment in the silence, then looked over to where he thought he had seen the violent attack the night before. The dingy wall was scuffed and marred; his eyes locked on a section next to the old dresser where the wallpaper was discolored.

Daniel got up and crossed over for a closer look at the stain. It was some kind of splatter on the old wallpaper. Daniel gripped the edges of the dresser and leaned his weight into it. The old piece of furniture groaned loudly as it rumbled over the floor. He stood back, caught his breath and squinted down at the newly exposed wall. The stain was darker along the baseboard. He kneeled down and wiped the floor beneath. His fingers streaked through the heavy dust, wiping a clearer view of the old floor.

There was a deep dark stain in the wood.

A cold feeling crept over Daniel. He ran his fingers back over to the old stain. It was black-brown. Not paint. Not varnish or oil wood stain. It was something else. Something more organic that had permeated the wood and had surfaced again over time.

It was an old bloodstain.

NINE

THE MIDDAY SUNLIGHT flickered through the rusted iron girders of the bridge over the Atchafalaya River; the truck tires hummed loudly on the metal grate decking. Daniel adjusted the truck visor to block the strobing sunlight effect. As he reached the other side of the bridge, he entered Krotz Springs.

It was a remarkably unremarkable little town: a collection of basic-needs businesses on one main street along the river. "Quaint" wasn't the first thought that came to mind, as Daniel slowed his truck and scanned the businesses. Everything had a corrugated metal roof, with either brick or concrete walls. Function definitely followed form here. Humidity, heat, and the threat of hurricanes and flooded swampland dictated what would survive.

Daniel was almost at the other end of the short main street when he pulled over. He consulted a page he had torn from an old phone book he had found at the house: "St. Landry Parish *Gazette*, 1209 Main St., Krotz Springs."

He looked up from the page and out at the businesses along the main drag. How could he have missed something as obvious as a newspaper office on a single main street? There was a thrift store and pharmacy in front of him; the faded address on the pharmacy read 1205 Main.

At least he was close. Daniel shut off the engine and climbed out of the truck. He started down the uneven sidewalk that alternated between asphalt and concrete. Clearly, no one was out to win any civic pride awards here.

He reached the building that should have been 1209. It was a butcher shop, Krotz Springs Choice Cuts. Shit. The *Gazette* must have moved.

Daniel stepped inside. The shop was air conditioned, thank god. Daniel breathed in the sticky sweet smell of fresh blood and raw meat. Behind the counter was a wiry middle-aged butcher with oval glasses, gray hair in a ponytail, and a beard. He was wrapping up some sausage. Once a hippie, always a hippie, Daniel thought.

The butcher placed the package on the counter and addressed a hunch-backed old African-American woman.

"There you go. Quarter-pound blood sausage. Four twenty."

The gnarled old woman fished a twenty out of her purse and slid it over to the butcher.

"Outta twenty," the butcher said, as he wiped his hands on his apron and went to the register. Daniel took the opportunity to move into the butcher's sight line. The butcher shot a glance at Daniel as he keyed in the purchase. "Help you with something?"

"Yeah, I was wondering if you could tell me where the St. Landry Parish *Gazette* moved to. It's the local paper."

The butcher counted back change to the twisted old woman, "That's five, ten and twenty. Thank you, Rae Lynn."

"See you next week, Zachary," she said, as she stuffed the wad of bills into her purse and grabbed her sausage. "Sure glad you're open on a Sunday; it's the only day I can get into town."

The butcher looked at Daniel as the old woman exited the shop. "You got it," he said.

"Got what?" Daniel asked, perplexed.

"The *Gazette*. What can I do for you?"

Daniel looked around the butcher shop. "This is the *Gazette* office?"

"Zachary Brandt, senior editor," he said, as he extended his hand.

Daniel tentatively shook the lean man's hand; it was clammy and cold.

"You were expecting the *New York Times*?"

"No, I just wouldn't have guessed, that's all. I mean, in a butcher shop like this."

Zachary smiled and strolled toward the back of the shop. "Personal ad?"

"Huh? No," Daniel answered as he followed, "No. Actually I was looking for back issues."

Zachary pushed through a hanging bead partition and into a small, cluttered office space. A plump, sweet-looking woman in her mid 50s was busy on her computer at the desk.

"Marla, we got someone lookin' to do some research."

The cherub-faced woman smiled at Daniel. "Of course, sure. Squeeze on in here."

"It's a twenty-dollar fee," Zachary added. "For handling and re-filing." The front door of the shop jingled as a new customer entered. "Marla will take care of you," Zachary said, and he moved back into the shop to help the new arrival.

"Can I get you some coffee, honey?"

"That'd be great," Daniel smiled back.

The little woman steered her squat body over to the filing cabinet where there was a coffee pot and cups on top, "Cream? Sugar?"

"Black."

Marla poured Daniel a cup. "What kind of research are you doing?"

"I'm looking into missing persons reports."

"Missing persons" she repeated, then handed him the coffee. "Here you go, sweetie."

"Thanks."

"Well, there haven't been a lot of them around here. Usually, someone goes missing, it's the gators that got 'em, and by the time we find what's left of them, well, it ain't pretty, but what's left ain't missin' no more." She opened a narrow closet door and snapped on the light. Inside were stacks of old file boxes. "We got all the issues going back about thirty years. Dates are on the boxes."

"That's a lot of issues," Daniel said as he stepped up to the closet.

"Fifty-two a year for the past fourteen years. It was a monthly before that," Marla said proudly, then pulled a stack of papers off the end of her desk. "Weekly now. That's why we're here on a Sunday, working. You can sit right here. Make yourself comfortable." Marla gave him another warm smile, then she pushed out the beaded curtain and went into the butcher shop.

Daniel took a sip of his coffee and stepped into the closet. He scanned the dates on the boxes until he found the issues from a decade earlier, the time frame after the final entry in Claire's diary. It would be a place to start. He grabbed one and slid it out.

———

WHACK! WHACK! WHACK! A rhythmic chopping sound drifted through the little office from an adjacent workroom behind the shop. Daniel sighed, rubbed his tired eyes and took the last sip of his coffee. He closed a *Gazette* issue and put it back into the open file box on the desk. It was the latest in a long string of issues that had turned up nothing helpful. Daniel checked the time on the computer screen on the cluttered desk. He'd been at this for over an hour, but it seemed like a lot longer.

WHACK! WHACK! WHACK! Daniel looked through the partially open door of the adjoining workroom. It was a long, narrow room with sides of beef and a couple of whole pigs hanging along one wall and a cutting table on the other. A man in his mid 30s in a blood-covered apron was working away on a large piece of beef. The plastic name tag on his apron read "Cliff." The man's features were familiar: Long nose, square jaw, round eyes. Genetics don't lie. He had to be the butcher's son, Daniel decided, and of course his name was Cliff. He looked like a Cliff. Tall. Oafish.

The freezer door banged open behind Cliff and another man entered, hefting a whole pig with the head still on. He dropped the carcass on the table and grabbed a saw. He was a thinner, wirier man. He was about Cliff's age and his name tag read "Alex." He grabbed a fine-toothed saw from a rack. Daniel had to look away when Alex started sawing through the rubbery pig's neck.

Daniel got up, stretched, and poured himself another cup of coffee. It was just on the border of tasting burned. He sat back down and pulled out the next issue from the file box. Sipping the coffee, he started flipping through the paper. Most of the stories in this issue were about the St. Landry Parish fair that had closed the week before. There were names and pictures of locals who had won various and forgettable awards. Daniel reached the end of the edition and closed it. Shit. This was getting tedious.

A peal of laughter rolled in from the butcher room. Daniel looked over and saw Cliff giggling at Alex, who was holding the severed pig's head down at his crotch, pumping his hips into it, mimicking oral sex.

Jesus Christ. Really? This is what goes on? Daniel was about to look away when Alex glanced at him through the partially open door. Daniel froze as their eyes locked. He was strangely embarrassed for the wiry butcher. But instead of being embarrassed,

Alex kept smiling his smug smile. His expression was almost challenging.

It was Daniel who looked away, unnerved. What the fuck kind of town was this? He took another sip of coffee, turned his attention back to the file box, and pulled out the next edition.

And that's when he found it.

A banner headline screamed across the top of the edition, "Local Girl Found Murdered."

Daniel set his coffee on the desk and unfolded the edition. As the lower half of the paper came into view, he saw a grainy black-and-white photograph on the lower left side of the page.

It was Claire.

TEN

A CHILL SHOT straight to Daniel's core. Everything in the world stopped dead. His eyes locked on the picture.

A moment passed, then another. What was staring back at Daniel was far more than he thought he'd find here.

Or was it?

Who was he bullshitting? This was exactly what he thought he would find. Only now that it was right in front of him, it seemed much more unreal, even dream-like.

The world around Daniel started to move again, and Cliff's rhythmic chopping filled his ears once more. He read the caption under the story: "Claire Waynright found stabbed to death in her home." He scanned the article for more details. "Eighteen years old, recent high school graduate, body found by her parents when they returned home, only child...."

He shifted his focus back to the photo. It was Claire's senior high school picture, and she was smiling. A radiant smile. Her braces were gone, and her eyes sparkled. Yes. No doubt. She was definitely the girl who had showed up at the house two nights in a row.

Daniel's mind began to race. What did it all mean? As strange as it seemed, there appeared to be only one explanation. But was he ready to accept it? Would he try to tell someone? How would it sound to someone else? It would be too strange even to try to explain. After all, he had been alone in that house. No one else had seen her, and when the police had come all they found were empty beer cans, and....

"Well, now, that wasn't a missing person, but it sure was a real tragedy," Marla's voice chimed in.

Daniel looked up and saw the squat woman peering over his shoulder. "Never caught who did it," she went on. "Police said it was most likely one of the drifters we get hitchin' through town. She lived with her parents off the highway about six miles down the road from town. Big house. Still there, just like it was. But there hasn't been anyone in it for years. Parents moved away shortly after she died; couldn't stand to stay there. I heard someone just bought it."

"Yeah, I know," Daniel interrupted. "Do you have a copier?"

"Sure. You can use this one with my computer right here. Twenty five cents a page."

"That's fine." Daniel folded back the page, placed it on the copier glass, and pressed the button. It was the only thing he could think to do with it. He knew he couldn't let it go. Too many things had gone missing before his eyes. He needed to hold onto this tightly.

Daniel stared numbly at the copy of the article as it trembled out of the scanner.

———

Moments later, Daniel stepped out of the butcher shop in a daze. He paused, looked down at the copy of Claire's article, then folded it in half. He continued down the uneven sidewalk to his truck and became aware of a flickering red light.

A Krotz Springs police cruiser was parked next to his truck. A stocky police deputy in his early 30s stood behind the tailgate, jotting down Daniel's license plate number.

"Is there a problem?"

The deputy kept his eyes on the plate as he continued to write. "No problem here," he said lazily.

"Is there a reason you're taking down my license number?"

The deputy raised his heavy black eyebrows and looked up at Daniel. He had a thick neck and a body-builder's physique. His arms were large, covered with black hair that seemed to cover every inch of his body except his square clean-shaven face. The nametag on his sweat-ringed khaki shirt told Daniel that this was Officer Bleeker. Is there anyone in Krotz Springs who doesn't have a job with a nametag? Daniel thought as he gazed back at the deputy's impassive face.

"It's just what we do here, that's all," Bleeker explained smugly. "We like to keep track of who's in the area. You working down at the old Waynright place?"

"Yeah, doin' a remodel job."

"My colleague tells me you had a visitor out there the other night. Some kind of assault victim?"

"Well, I thought I had, but..." Daniel trailed off, deliberating what to say next.

"Now you're not so sure?" Bleeker furrowed his thick eyebrows.

Daniel regarded the bull-like man for a moment, then decided he didn't owe him an explanation. "Look, I'm sorry, I've got to get to work," he said. Daniel stepped past him to his truck.

Bleeker slowly folded his notebook closed, "FYI, don't try drivin' and drinkin' around here. We have a zero tolerance policy. Zeero. This ain't New Orleans. We like to keep our roads safe."

"Glad to hear it," Daniel said as he climbed behind the wheel. He started his truck and pulled away. He glanced in the rearview at Bleeker as the deputy strolled back to his cruiser. What the fuck was it with the cops in this town? First the old guy the other night and now this wanna-be pro wrestler asshole. Since when did paranoia replace good old southern hospitality?

Daniel turned onto the bridge, and his mind went back to Claire. He still couldn't quite accept what his gut was telling him. Was there something he was overlooking? Maybe he had been drinking a lot more than he thought and had imagined both visits. And the stain. What made him think it was blood?

Daniel roared off the bridge and started down the winding road. He had been alone for a long time. Maybe he had been drifting away. Little by little losing his mind. There was no real way to check himself. If a tree falls in the woods and no one's around.... After all, he had never been alone like this for so long. Maybe we need someone around to check on us more than we think we do. Maybe sanity is much more fragile than we want to believe.

All the way back to the house, Daniel's thoughts kept churning. He had to figure out what to do next. His mind wouldn't be quiet. It kept going in circles, and he was becoming exhausted. He needed a drink. A beer.

He heard himself sigh as he pulled into the dirt driveway. Good. One thing at a time. First a drink, then he could try to figure this out.

Eileen Cho's Mercedes was parked in front of the house.

ELEVEN

THE COLORFUL WOMAN was standing on the porch as Daniel climbed out of his truck and approached.

"Eileen?" He could see that her usually sunny expression was absent; instead, there was a haunted, frightened look on her face.

"Where have you been?" she asked.

"In town," he said, as he climbed the porch.

"Are you okay?"

"Yeah. Yeah, I'm fine. What're you doing here?"

Cho approached him, keeping her eyes locked on his. "I had to see you. To be sure."

Daniel paused, frowning. "You came all the way down here just to see if I was okay?"

Cho looked away from him, "Yes. I mean, no. Not exactly. I...."

Daniel studied the anxious woman for a moment. "Come on inside."

He pulled open the screen, unlocked the door, and pushed it open. Cho hesitated, then stepped past him and into the house.

Cho stopped outside the plastic sheeting in the entryway. Daniel came up behind her and yanked it aside. "As you can see,

I'm knee deep in it. Go ahead." He gestured; she took a shallow breath and stepped through the plastic and into the living room.

She paused again, scanning the demolition.

"I'm doin' pretty good with the schedule, I think," Daniel said. "The local guy I got working seems to be pulling his weight okay. If you want to look upstairs...."

"I couldn't sleep last night, Daniel," she interrupted. "I couldn't stop thinking about this place. And you."

"Me?"

She turned back to face him. "It was an awful feeling. I don't know what it all means, but...." She trailed off, took a shaky breath and steadied her nerves. "I'm beginning to think having you here is a terrible mistake."

"What're you talking about?" Now it was Daniel's turn to be anxious. Was she firing him?

But Cho's mind was somewhere else. Somewhere different. She approached him again, focused and concerned. "Daniel, if there's been something going on here, please, for your own good, you've got to tell me."

Her plea hung in the silence. Daniel couldn't help himself; he looked away, avoiding her eye contact. Even as he was doing it, he knew it was a stupid move. No matter what he thought of her New Age feng shui bullshit, he could tell that she could read people. And right now everything he had been going through was silently pouring out of him.

"Daniel?" Cho's voice was insistent now.

Daniel hesitated, his back partially turned to her. He felt trapped. But not by her. He had done it to himself. Maybe on purpose. Some-place deep down, Daniel had known she would be the only person in the world to whom he could even begin to try to explain what he had been through and what he had found in Krotz Springs.

"I don't know what it is, exactly," Daniel heard himself say. "It always starts with things missing. Small stuff, not where I left it. Then I hear her scream."

"Who?" Cho asked, trying to contain her alarm.

Daniel took another moment; he knew there was no turning back now. He had to lay it all out there and hope for the best. "Claire. Her name's Claire. I see her running up the driveway. I talk to her. But it's different each time. She doesn't remember me from the time before. Then last night, in the room, I saw her get...." Daniel's voice went dry. He swallowed, took a shallow breath, and continued with difficulty. "I found blood stains, old, from years ago. I just came back from town, where I found this." He pulled out the copy of the article about Claire's murder and unfolded it.

Cho stared for a moment at the grainy picture of Claire, "Oh, god," she whispered, stunned. Her feelings had been right.

Eileen Cho had been seven years old when she had the first encounter she could remember. It happened outside of their Hong Kong apartment on Robinson Road above the botanical gardens. Their apartment was on the third floor of a five-story building that faced the city and harbor below. Eileen was awakened by a blaring horn and the screech of tires. There were muffled voices outside. When she tried to get up, her father told her to go back to bed. But things only got louder. She could hear her mother start to cry. More cars outside. Sirens.

When Eileen came out of her room, she saw her mother on the couch in tears and her father trying to comfort her. Two policemen were standing nearby. A car in front of the house had hit Uncle Lin, and he was dead. She learned much later that he had been drinking, had parked his car down the winding street, and was staggering home. Another car came out of nowhere and killed him instantly.

But it was Eileen's encounter two weeks after the accident that changed her life forever. She was asleep when she heard the same car tires screech. She bolted awake. But the apartment was dark and silent this time. She walked out of her bedroom and was heading to her parents' room on the other side of the big front window. There, she hesitated. She felt something draw her to the window. When she looked down, she saw her uncle standing on the side of the road across the street. She froze, looking at him intently. He looked up at her with a distant smile on his face.

Eileen immediately ran to her parents' room and woke them. Her voice raced as she told them that Uncle Lin was outside. But her parents' faces told her more than any words could. Her mother gently took her into her arms and consoled her. Uncle Lin is dead, she told her. Uncle Lin is gone. From the tone of her mother's voice, Eileen knew she couldn't say anything more about what she had seen.

From then on, she kept her encounters to herself. She talked herself into believing they were nothing but her imagination. It wasn't until she was in high school that she began to "listen" to her feelings. She met a schoolmate who had the same sensitivity. The topic of their shared ability first came up innocuously at a late-night slumber party after a stolen bottle of her parents' wine had been consumed. Their other friends were asleep, and Eileen and the girl bonded over their experiences. It seemed less frightening to Eileen to know there was someone like her who had the same sensitivity.

As the years went by, Eileen grew more comfortable with her sensitivity and even managed to find a career that suited her skills. After college, she started working as an interior designer with her father's architectural firm in Hong Kong. Later, her success and fame brought her to America, where she had done well.

She originally had had a feeling about Daniel when they first talked on the phone. It seemed as if their meeting was destiny rather than a routine job interview, and even in that first conversation, she could sense that Daniel was disconnected. He was drifting, not engaged with this world, the way most of us are.

———

Daniel watched Cho's face as she stared at the newspaper picture in silence. He expected that she would either dismiss all of this immediately or embrace it, but her delayed reaction was far more troubling. He said, "I'm not someone who believes in ghosts, but this, I can't explain."

Cho looked up at him. This wasn't a ghost. Not exactly. As least not the kind of ghost Cho had grown to understand. "This isn't a residual phantom loop," she said. "I mean, it's not a ghost the way you're talking about. You wouldn't be able to change what happened if it were. You wouldn't be able to talk to her." Cho turned and took in the demolished room. "The house...all the changes we made," she went on. "The energy flow here is different now. I've never sensed it so strongly before. We have opened something up and released a flow that had been sealed for years." She thought for a moment, then looked back at Daniel. "What about your missing things? After she's gone, do the missing things return?

"They're right back where I left them."

"Like they've never been moved?"

"That's right."

Cho took a careful moment to consider what she was beginning to form in her mind. Everything seemed to be pointing in one direction.

"Time," she said.

"Time?" She had thrown him another curve ball. This wasn't

what Daniel was expecting at all. A ghost, a haunting, maybe, but not "time."

"Yes. Time. Things would disappear because they didn't exist here in an earlier time. They'd return again when you came back to the present."

"*Me?*"

Cho nodded slowly.

"You think *I'm* going back in time?"

"Partially, yes. It would explain how you're able to interact with the people there and change what happened."

"But the house," Daniel said. "When she's here, it looks the same to me. The dust covers, the construction."

"It would, to you." It was all starting to come into focus to Cho now. Changing the flow of energy by moving the walls normally wouldn't be enough for someone to become unstuck in time, but Daniel was different. He was already unstuck. He had let go of his life here. He was drifting through it, and that had made him susceptible to the encounters.

"Your grip here in our world is tenuous, but not completely gone, Daniel," she said. "That's why anything you're carrying or wearing stays with you when you slip partially into the past. It's like you're in two places at once."

Daniel took a shaky breath. "Shit. And I was having trouble with the ghost idea."

"Look, I know what this sounds like, but there really is a theory behind it. The right-brainers call it Quantum Physics. Wormholes. Alternative time lines, that sort of thing."

Daniel slowly sat on the couch. Cho could tell this wasn't going down well with him. She knew she had to tell him more so that he would understand it the way she was beginning to understand. But she didn't want to tell him everything. She went to sit next to him and gently placed her hand on his knee. "I know about your wife, Daniel. You lost the one person you loved, and now there's nothing holding you here. You have no place to belong. That's why you're so much more vulnerable to time shifts than other people."

Daniel took a moment to absorb this; he needed to understand exactly what it all meant. She was telling him that Claire wasn't a ghost. She was real, and what he had encountered had been real, but in a different time.

Daniel knew the next question he had to ask. "If both times I was with her, and things were different because of me, does it mean that I can change things back then? Things that don't have to happen?"

Cho felt her entire body tense. She should have seen this coming, especially from Daniel. "Daniel, you won't find what you're looking for back there. This is your time, here. Now is where you belong. You should leave this house immediately. You should get out now."

"Leave?"

"Of course. If you stay here, it could happen again. And if you slip back in time again, it could be fatal. Everything that happens to you back there is real. The danger is real. You could be killed just as easily as she was."

Cho's words hung in the silence for a moment. The fear in her voice was unlike anything he had ever heard from her before.

TWELVE

Daniel placed his toolbox into the back of his pick-up, where he had already packed his other things. Cho stood nearby, shielding her eyes as she squinted at him in the afternoon sunlight. "I'll make sure Reggie gets hired on with your replacement," she said.

Daniel turned to her, wiping his hands on his pants. "Thanks."

"And call me later, when you get someplace safe."

"I will."

They stood for a moment as the iridescent sound of the cicadas wafted through the humid air. She reached over and hugged him. "This is the right thing to do, Daniel. Moving on is the right thing to do."

Daniel felt strangely comfortable in the woman's arms; her maternal and caring feelings for him were palpable. He pulled away. "Yeah, well, moving on is something I'm used to doin'," he said. And he meant it. In the last few hours, as he had packed up his things, the old familiar feelings had returned to him. He was sliding back into the gray fog that hung over his life, and even though it came with a constant sadness, it was familiar and strangely comforting. He smiled faintly at Cho and climbed into his truck.

"Don't forget to call me," she reminded him.

"I'll remember," he said as he started the engine and dropped it into gear. Cho gave him a final smile and a little wave as he pulled away down the driveway.

———

And so here he was again, facing another empty road ahead. About an hour out of Krotz Springs, the sun was hanging low as he sped down the Interstate, heading east this time. He figured he'd drift down to Florida, where he might be able to pick up some construction work. At least it would be warm in the winter if he lasted that long there. He had seen pictures of Orlando, and it seemed like a place with nothing but man-made destinations. The perfect place for construction workers like Daniel, and a big enough sprawl to get lost in.

Lost.

That's what it really was, wasn't it? During the silent drive, the truth had bubbled up and revealed itself. He was looking to get lost again.

Daniel held on to the realization for a moment. It seemed to crystallize all the feelings he had had in the year since Angie's death. It gave a name to the gray fog he was re-entering.

But then, without any warning, a new feeling took him by surprise. It was a restless, troubled feeling.

He was wrong. Dead wrong. This time was different. This time he wasn't looking to get lost. This time he was running.

Shit. Daniel snapped out of his thoughts. There was an exit in front of him.

He took it.

As he slowed to a stop at the end of the ramp, he realized that he wasn't sure what he was doing. He took an anxious breath, pulled over to the side, and put the truck in park.

There. He was still. He wasn't moving. He wasn't going forward and he wasn't going back. He wasn't running and he wasn't getting lost. And that only begged the question: Where was he?

Of course, his eyes told him he was in the middle of some flat, anonymous part of Louisiana, far north of the coast. But his feelings were telling him something different. He struggled to find the wellspring for this strange new condition that had overtaken him: if he felt like he was running, it had to be that there was something to run from. And if he was running from something, it had to mean that, for the first time in a long time, he had found something.

That was it. The moment he formed the words in his head, his throat tightened involuntarily. He felt his heart thump in his chest.

Daniel looked down at the seat next to him. The copy of Claire's article was tucked under an old road map.He reached down, slid the copy out from under the map, and unfolded it.

There she was again. Claire. Smiling back at him from the grainy black-and-white graduation picture.

She was what he had found. She was his purpose.

Daniel stayed there on the side of the road in his truck, staring at the picture for what seemed like an eternity—an eternity that collapsed all time and distance. Why would he run from this when he had nowhere to run? Why should he care if it could cost him his life when he had no real life to live?

There was no one else who could go back and save Claire. Just him. With Angie, he had felt helpless, but this was different. He could do this. He could save her. And if he didn't, she would remain dead forever.

The gray fog was long gone now. Everything seemed crystal clear to Daniel.

He dropped the truck back into gear and hit the gas. He circled under the Interstate and started back to Krotz Springs.

Back to his destiny.

———

A couple of hours later, the sun had faded below the tangled tree line of the bayou. The early evening air was alive once more with the sounds of impending night. The headlights from Daniel's truck swung up the driveway to the house in the dusky light. He squinted at the surrounding yard and barn. No sign of Cho. She had left, just as she had said she would, hours ago.

Daniel pulled his truck to a stop outside the wrought-iron fence and shut off the engine. He glanced down at several large Wal-Mart bags. He had stopped on his way back to get some routine supplies, along with one special item.

He snapped off his headlights, gathered the large bags, and climbed out. He paused a moment, looking up at the silent, empty house that loomed in front of him, then pushed through the gate and headed up the walkway.

He dumped the bags on the porch and tried the door. Cho had locked it. He looked around, found a heavy rock in the weed-choked garden off the side of the porch, and approached the corner pane of the front window. He grimaced and slammed the rock against the window. The dirty old glass shattered easily. He tossed the rock aside and reached in to unlock the latch, careful not to cut himself on the shards.

Moments later, he was back inside. He snapped on the bare overhead light and scanned the demolished room. It was just as he had left it. He checked his watch. It was six-thirty. Still a bit early.

Not completely dark out yet. He had time to learn more about what he might be facing.

He went upstairs, snapped on the hall light, and crossed to the corner pink room. Claire's room.

He took the copy of Claire's article out of his pocket and checked the date. June 12 2000. He stepped through the open wall and went back to the boxes of her belongings. He pulled open the box he had looked through before and took out her diary. He flipped all the way to the end.

Claire's last entry. Her neat, cursive writing spelled out the date: June 2. Daniel eased himself down on the edge of the dresser. If there was anything here to help him learn what he would be confronting tonight, he needed to see it.

"Senior year was going to be the best. Three years in this place and it's all Cindy and I ever talked about. Now all she talks about is Brian. I want to be nice about it, but it's so hard. Sometimes I think I'll never find someone like she has. I mean, I don't know how it's supposed to happen. How do people find each other? God, I wish senior year would end. Mom and Dad are gone this weekend to New Orleans. I'm going to go out to The Villa tonight and see what kind of trouble I can get into."

Daniel turned the page. There was nothing else. The article had said that Claire's parents were gone when she was killed. This had to be it. This had to have been written the weekend she was killed.

Daniel looked back at the last sentence once more. Pieces were beginning to fit together. He had seen a hole-in-the-wall bar on the way out of Krotz Springs named "The Villa." If she had gone there that night, it would have been one of the last places she had been seen alive. She could have been drinking. Met someone there.

Daniel considered this for a moment. She hadn't seemed drunk at all when he saw her, either time. Daniel set the diary back into the box and slid it closed. He had to check himself; he was connecting too many dots that didn't necessarily connect. The article said her parents had discovered her body when they returned. It didn't say how long she might have been dead. That meant he didn't know for sure if her last diary entry had been written the same night she had been killed. It could have been one, two, or even three nights before.

Daniel sighed. Playing detective wasn't his strong suit, and besides, this wasn't a mystery he was here to solve. He knew the killer would be right behind Claire. No mystery about it.

Enough fucking around. He needed to cover his tracks with Cho. He took out his cell phone and dialed her number. It went right to voice mail, and Daniel sighed, relieved. He wouldn't have to field any probing questions. "Eileen. It's Daniel. Just wanted to tell you I'm on the road. Heading east. I'm gonna see how far I can get tonight before I grab a hotel." Daniel paused, planning the next words of his lie, then continued. "Thanks for all your help with this. I really appreciate it."

He punched off. Good. Nice touch. It would keep her at bay, at least for tonight.

Daniel looked out the bedroom window. It was dark now. Time to get this started.

Daniel worked quickly to set the scene. He placed his cell phone on his toolbox by the couch. He set his duffle bag on the end of the bed in the guest room. He even placed a beer can on the cross brace in the open wall to Claire's room. He didn't know what might have made a difference, and he didn't want to take a chance tonight. He wanted things to be as close to the way they had been both times she had shown up.

But there was one big exception this time.

Daniel reached into the large Wal-Mart bag and pulled out a long cardboard box. He flipped open the lid and took out his insurance.

A shotgun.

He pumped the action. Clean. Brand new. He reached back into the bag and took out a fresh box of shells. He slid six into the chamber.

There. He was ready.

He climbed the stairs with the gun and crossed down the hall to Claire's room. He stepped in, pulled a large wooden box up to the window, and put the shotgun in his lap. This was his best vantage point. He'd be able to see her coming from here.

He sat back, exhaled slowly, and whispered to himself with complete resolve, "Okay. Let's get this right this time."

<h1 style="text-align:center">THIRTEEN</h1>

FOUR HOURS LATER, Daniel was awakened by Claire's faint, desperate cry. His eyes snapped open and he bolted upright. Shit. He had dozed off. But when? It didn't matter. Daniel looked over at the cross brace in the open wall.

The beer can was gone.

Another desperate cry came from outside. It was closer this time. Daniel looked back out the window. Sure enough, Claire was stumbling up the driveway, clutching her wounded neck; she was covered in blood, just as she had been both other times.

Daniel leaped up, with the shotgun in his hands, and raced from the room. He clambered downstairs, glancing at the coffee table. His toolboxes were gone. Cell phone too. He frantically shoved his way through the plastic sheeting and threw open the front door.

Claire skidded to a stop in the driveway when she saw Daniel racing toward her. Her eyes went wide and she screamed.

"No. It's all right, I'm not going to hurt you!" Daniel slowed, realizing how this must look to her. He lowered the shotgun and opened his arms to her.

Claire backed away from him, terrified. Daniel shook the shotgun. "This is only to protect us," he said. "Claire, please, you've got to trust me. Your life depends on it."

Claire hesitated warily. "How do you know my name?"

Daniel had to think quickly; he couldn't explain everything now. The killer would be right behind her. "Look, I know you don't remember me, but we've met. I'm Daniel. Daniel Nash. Please. You've got to trust me. I know he's after you. I just want to protect you."

A branch cracked in the shadowy line of trees down the driveway. He was coming. Daniel extended his hand to her. "Hurry, please. I don't want him to see me."

The world was spinning fast around Claire. She looked down at the stranger's extended hand. How did he know she was being chased? If she went with him, would he also harm her? The heavy footsteps cracked louder through the brush behind her. She knew what was behind her, and she knew it was bad. She didn't have a choice. She grabbed Daniel's hand.

"Good. Good, come on," he said.

They hurried back up the walkway and into the house. Daniel slammed and locked the door behind them. He turned back to Claire. "Here." Once again, he steered Claire to the couch and uncovered it. "Stay right here. I'm not gonna give him a chance to get into the house." Daniel hurried back to the front window and pulled the curtain aside. He peered out the shattered windowpane.

Sure enough, the silhouette of the killer emerged from the dark bayou, heading their way. Daniel wiped the sweat from his eyes with his arm and racked the shotgun. He raised the weapon, nestled the stock into his shoulder, and squinted down the barrel at the approaching killer.

The dark form grew closer, striding determinedly toward the

house; the knife in his hand glinted in the moonlight. Daniel took a deep breath and steadied his aim. The killer slowed his pace as he reached the outside of the wrought-iron gate. Daniel's finger tightened on the trigger. He closed one eye and lined up the bead at the end of the barrel with the killer in the distance. It was now or never.

BOOM! The deafening shotgun blast rolled through the living room. Claire clutched her ears and cried out.

Outside, at the edge of the yard, the killer reeled back in a flurry of blood. His body crashed back through the gate and slammed to the ground.

Daniel opened his eye and lifted his head from the shotgun. The body was motionless, sprawled on the ground just outside the gate. Daniel looked over at Claire, who cringed on the couch. She removed her hands from her ears.

"It's okay. I got him." Daniel turned away from the window. "Wait here. Don't go anywhere."

Claire nodded and gave a slight gasp.

"Are you okay?"

Claire nodded again. "Yeah. Yeah." She was okay, but terrified.

Daniel twisted the front door lock and pulled it open. He steadied his nerves, stepped outside, and crossed the porch. He paused, squinting out to the end of the walkway at the lifeless form. A rivulet of glistening blood ran down the path by the gate. He raised the shotgun waist high in front of him and made his way down the steps and out the walk.

As Daniel drew closer, he could see that the fallen killer was face down in the damp dirt. Daniel raised the shotgun to eye level and stopped, standing over the body. He studied the form in the darkness, looking for any signs of life, careful to keep the shotgun aimed and ready. The body remained motionless.

Daniel lifted his left foot, placed it on the killer's side, and gave it a firm nudge. The body rocked limply back and forth, then went still again. Daniel yelled back at the dark house, "Claire! It's okay! I got him!"

Daniel gathered his courage and slid his boot under the torso. He grimaced and shoved with all his might. The body turned awkwardly, teetered on its side for a moment, then flopped over onto its back. Daniel's eyes snapped to the face. Even through the smeared blood and mud, what Daniel saw was familiar. The killer's nose was long and thin, his jaw was square and the eyes were round.

The butcher's son.

At least ten years younger than when Daniel had seen him before, but recognizable. Cliff. That was the name on the tag, Daniel remembered. Daniel looked down at Cliff's arm.

Cliff's hand was blown off at the wrist.

Daniel recoiled, sickened by the gruesome carnage. He took a step back, and his foot landed on something squishy. Daniel looked down. It was the severed hand.

"Jesus fuck!" Daniel kicked the bloody appendage away and started scraping his boot on the edge of the brick walkway. The tattered bits of flesh clung to the deep treads of his work boot. He shook his boot and kicked it once, twice, against the iron fence. The gore was tenacious. He would have to find a hose and spray it to get it out. Maybe even use a wire brush and try to scrape-

Cliff's eyes snapped open.

His good hand shot up with the hunting knife, swung around, and came down hard.

It sunk into Daniel's calf.

The searing pain shot up Daniel's leg. He screamed in agony and dropped the shotgun. BOOM! The shotgun blasted wildly as it hit the ground. Daniel crashed back against the fence, hyperventilating. He looked down at the gleaming blade lodged in his calf muscle.

Cliff slowly began to sit up. But Daniel's eyes were locked on the knife in his calf; he reached down with a trembling hand and grabbed the handle. He grimaced and yanked the blade out, accidentally twisting it in the process. Another jolt of excruciating pain shot up his body. He gasped and clutched the fence to prevent him from collapsing. He looked back at the fallen shotgun.

Cliff was on his feet, staggering toward the gun.

Daniel launched himself off the fence, dove down, and grabbed the shotgun first. He swung the barrel around with all his might, cracking Cliff in the shin. Cliff flailed backward.

Daniel frantically turned the shotgun around, his bloody fingers slipping on the barrel. He gripped the pump hard and racked a shell into the chamber, then whipped around just in time to see Cliff hobbling toward the corner of the house, clutching his bleeding stump tightly at the wrist.

BOOM! Daniel's shot was careless, unthinking. The buckshot ripped into the edge of the house, missing Cliff, who ducked out of sight around the side of the building. Daniel scrambled to his feet and took off after him.

Cliff clambered up the back steps to the kitchen door. He tried the knob with his good hand. It was locked. BOOM! Another shot rang out behind him. Daniel was closing in, and the shots were no longer careless. Cliff leaped off the back stoop and scrambled into the woods.

Daniel pumped another round into the chamber and hobbled after Cliff into the misty bayou. He scanned the shadowy maze of brush as he pushed along. There was no sign of blood. Shit. Had he lost him? Daniel reached the embankment to the deserted highway and paused. Nothing.

Daniel caught his breath. The shooting pain in his leg drew his attention to his wound. Daniel balanced the shotgun against a bald cypress and pulled off his belt. He cinched it just above the wound in his calf muscle.

CRACK! A branch snapped on the embankment several yards away. Daniel looked up just in time to see Cliff's shadow slip up onto the highway. Daniel snatched up the shotgun and took aim. But Cliff slid out of sight on the other side of the highway before he could get off a shot.

Daniel frantically climbed the embankment up to the highway, then hobbled across and down the other side. The branches whipped and lashed at him as he shoved through the tangled brush and came out on the river's edge. He looked up and down the bank. No sign of Cliff. He spun back around. Something dripping off the branches along the path caught his eye. Cliff's blood.

Daniel took off, following the dark crimson trail that led up the path. He raised his shotgun, getting ready for anything; he had to be gaining on Cliff by now.

Daniel rounded the bend and came upon the dilapidated boathouse. He paused and scanned the old shack. The trail of blood led across the rotted wood porch to the door. Daniel braced himself, positioning the shotgun into his shoulder. He stepped onto the porch. The old wood creaked. Daniel stopped and looked back at the shack. Nothing. It was still. Daniel took another step closer, keeping his eyes locked on the shed. A shadow passed between the cracks in the wood.

BOOM! Daniel ripped a hole in the rotting wall. Heavy footsteps thumped through the shack. There was another loud crack, followed by a heavy splash. Cliff had gone out the other side.

Daniel raced to the other end of the porch and looked down. A ripple ran across the surface of the black water under the boathouse. Daniel aimed the shotgun.

He waited. There was nothing more.

Daniel took a step back from the edge of the old porch. CRACK! The rotting wood gave way beneath him. The shotgun slipped from his hands. Daniel plunged downward though the rotting porch boards. At the last second, he grabbed the edge to stop his descent.

He clung tightly to the mossy old boards, with his body halfway through the hole and his legs submerged in the black water below. He looked over and saw the shotgun on the deck, inches away from his grip.

Daniel rallied his strength and started to pull himself back up. He made it a few inches before his hand slipped back on the mossy wood. He caught himself before going all the way into the water.

Shit. Now what? Daniel considered his options. The shotgun was out of reach on the deck above him. Should he let go, then swim around and come up and get it? That would mean leaving the shotgun unattended. Where was Cliff? Had he gotten away?

Daniel glanced down at the black water that his legs were submerged in. One thing was certain, staying here wasn't an option. He decided to make one more attempt. He took a deep breath and pulled with all his might. His arms burned. His fingers just managed to grab the shotgun barrel.

WHOOSH! Cliff burst up out of the black water beneath Daniel. He grabbed Daniel's leg with his good hand. Daniel kicked violently, then let go. They both plunged down into the water with an immense splash.

The rush of inner space swirled around Daniel. He couldn't see anything. He felt his feet sink into the muddy bottom, but he clung to the shotgun with all his strength and shoved up off the riverbed.

Daniel burst to the surface to see Cliff coming at him again. Daniel whipped the shotgun stock around and cracked Cliff in the face. Cliff flailed backward with a splash. Daniel leveled the barrel and fired. It was a wild shot.

Cliff dove under the black water. Daniel racked the shotgun and leveled it just above the water line, waiting for Cliff to surface.

A loud splash came from near the riverbank. Daniel spun around and saw Cliff scrambling out of the water. Daniel took aim. CLICK! Misfire.

Daniel waded painfully to the bank and climbed out. He racked the shotgun over and over, ejected the shells, and shook out the water. A few of the rounds didn't look too bad; the gunpowder was probably still dry in the plastic casings. He blew them dry, rubbed them in his hands, and reloaded.

———

Blood loss was beginning to make Cliff weak as he staggered up to the isolated road. He grimaced as he looked down at his tattered stump of a wrist, which he cradled in his other hand. The man with the shotgun was relentless. Where the fuck had he come from? Who was he? Everyone at The Villa knew that Claire's parents were out of town for the whole weekend. Maybe they'd come back early, and this was the father? Just his fucking luck. But he didn't think so. This man was younger.

Cliff looked down the road where Claire's Toyota was parked. Shattered glass from the window she had kicked out was all over the road. Fucking bitch. He knew he'd have to cut his losses now and try to deal with the fallout from all this. It would be his word against hers. The bitch had wanted it. Everyone at The Villa would back up his story.

Cliff staggered over to his Camaro, which was parked behind Claire's Toyota. He was relieved to see it was still there. But as he grew closer, a puzzled look crossed his face. His Camaro was empty. Shit. Where the hell was...?

BOOM!

A violent thump hit Cliff's chest. He felt his feet leave the ground. A blinding white flash was the last thing he saw.

Then blackness.

———

Daniel lowered the shotgun from his shoulder. It was a clean shot. Right in the chest. But he had known he couldn't take any chances. Daniel racked the shotgun again and staggered over to the fallen butcher's son. A pool of blood ebbed out around his body. Daniel took aim again.

BOOM! He blasted a second time. The man twitched slightly, then went still.

He was dead.

Daniel allowed himself to take a cleansing breath. "Now try killing her, you piece of shit."

He had done it. Three tries it had taken him, but he had done it. If Cho was right about the past, he had just created a new version of what had happened all those years ago. A new version, one in which Claire lived.

Daniel looked away from Cliff's body and over at Claire's Toyota and the Camaro parked on the lone stretch of road. If they were there, he was still back in time. And that meant that Claire was still back at the house.

The pain in Daniel's calf began to throb again. All the adrenaline that had been coursing through his body had begun to subside. Daniel turned and started down the isolated road. He followed it around a long bend until he reached the stretch behind the house. He went down the long embankment and through the brush, then staggered up to the back porch.

He hesitated and caught his breath. He looked down at his wounded calf. It was starting to go numb. He set the shotgun down and adjusted his makeshift tourniquet. At least he had stopped the bleeding. He would have to get to town and find someone to take a look at it. Daniel reached for the shotgun again.

Claire's blood-curdling scream came from inside the house.

FOURTEEN

No. It couldn't be.

Daniel shot a look up at the dark house. What the fuck was happening? There was a loud crash of glass from the living room.

Daniel grabbed the shotgun and hobbled up to the back door, "Claire!" He slammed his weight against the door. "Claire!" He reared back, slammed again. The old door cracked open. Daniel burst into the kitchen. It was dark. Quiet.

He paused, waiting for his eyes to adjust. Something felt different. There was no construction rubble in the kitchen. As Daniel's eyes grew used to the darkness, he looked toward the living room.

The wall was back in place.

A hand grabbed his good leg from behind. Daniel spun around. Claire was cowering behind the now polished kitchen counter. "He's in the living room," she whispered.

Daniel looked down at the terrified girl, puzzled. "Who?" This was impossible; he had killed Cliff and left him on the road back there.

A silhouette loomed in the kitchen doorway. Daniel whipped the shotgun up and squinted at the silhouetted man.

No. It wasn't Cliff. It was someone else.

He was shorter, wore a trucker's cap pulled down tight, and had taken the time to cover his face with a dirty T-shirt tied behind his neck.

BOOM! Daniel fired. The newcomer dove back into the living room. The buckshot shredded the doorjamb. Daniel looked back down at Claire. "Who is that?"

"The other one."

"What other one?"

"There were two of them that stopped."

"Two? What are you talking about? There are *two* men after you?"

"No, only one came after me. The other one was still in his car. I'm sure only one came after me. This one must have heard the gunshots."

Daniel felt himself go numb. What the fuck had he gotten himself into? This was too messy and complicated and happening too fast. Everything must have changed when he shot at Cliff in front of the house. Now this man was after them; the 'other one from the car,' and he was coming after them with his face covered. This was premeditated retaliation. Methodical. This man wasn't desperate and scared the way Cliff had been.

Daniel looked down at the shotgun and racked it again. The empty cartridge fluttered out, but the chamber didn't refill. Daniel frantically racked it again. Nothing. No more shells. The shotgun was empty.

"Fuck." He had left the box of shells in the living room on the coffee table. Daniel reached over and pulled a knife from the butcher block on the counter. "Stay behind me," he said to Claire.

Claire rose from her place behind the counter and grabbed Daniel's shirt. They crept across the kitchen. "Is anyone else home tonight?" Daniel whispered to her.

"No. My parents went to—"

"New Orleans. Right. I forgot."

"How did you—?"

"Shhh."

They reached the kitchen door. Daniel signaled her to stay behind the wall, and he peered out into the living room. Everything was different. The entryway wall was back in place. The furniture was neatly arranged. It was clean. It was lived in. A calendar hung on the nearby refrigerator. It was open to August, 2000.

"Jesus," Daniel whispered. There was only one explanation. He had let go of his time completely; he was now firmly back in the year 2000.

Daniel looked at the coffee table, where he had left the box of shotgun shells. Of course they weren't there. He had the gun only because he had had it on his lap as he sat in front of the window. Everything else was back in the present. Or was it the future? Daniel set the empty shotgun down and raised his knife. It would have to do. It was all he had.

Daniel scanned the room, then put his finger to his lips and nodded to Claire to come with him.

Daniel gripped the knife as they crept into the living room. Claire clung to him. "Where's the phone?" he asked.

"Over there, by the stairs," she whispered back.

They went over to a small alcove by the stairs, and Daniel picked up the phone. There was no dial tone. "Dead," he whispered to Claire.

"The lights went out when you were gone. He must have cut the phone line too," she whispered back.

Daniel was about to drop the phone back onto the cradle when it happened.

The man plunged straight down from staircase above, tackling Daniel.

They crashed to the floor, knocking Claire aside. The man

smashed Daniel across the face with the phone, then wrapped the cord around his neck. Daniel clawed at the tightening wire, gasping for air.

Claire staggered to her feet, grabbed a nearby chair, and swung it. Its wooden legs shattered as they smashed into the man. He tumbled back, releasing the cord around Daniel's neck. Daniel coughed and gulped for air as he leaped up and slashed the knife across the man's forearm. The man hollered in pain as he staggered back toward the front door and fumbled for the knob. Daniel launched himself after him just as he was going out the door. The man reeled around and slammed the door on Daniel's hand. Daniel cried out and let go.

The man dove off the front porch and raced out the gate. Daniel burst out after him, clutching his bleeding hand; he looked up just in time to see the man grab a rusted ax off the woodpile outside the barn and take off down the driveway.

Claire hurried out the door behind Daniel. "The car," she said. "He's going back to his car."

Daniel started down the walkway. Claire followed. "Wait!" she cried. Daniel skidded to a stop and turned back, but Claire grabbed him. "Just let him go."

Daniel looked down at the frightened girl clinging to his arm. "I can't. If there's even a chance he'll come back for you, I can't."

Claire stared into the eyes of the stranger who had saved her life. A million questions raced through her mind: How did he know everything about her? How did he get here? Who was he?

Daniel started to pull away from her again. "Where did you come from?" she asked. It was a place for her to start. At least he could tell her that much.

Daniel knew her question was inevitable. He knew he'd have to give her some kind of story, and he was ready. "I was hitch hiking," he told her. "I found a place to camp out down the road. I heard your screams." Daniel could see by the confusion in her eyes that there were going to be more questions coming, and this wasn't the time to answer them. "Look. Trust me, please. You have to trust me. I know what I'm doing. I'll explain later. He's getting away."

Claire took a shaky breath and let go of his arm. "All right," she said. "I know a short cut back to the part of the road where the cars are parked. We can get there before he does."

———

Moments later, Daniel and Claire emerged from the bayou at the edge of the isolated road. The Camaro was still parked behind her Toyota. Cliff's body was lying face down in a large pool of blood. Claire choked back a nauseous reaction and looked away from the carnage.

"Which car is yours?" Daniel asked, as he scanned the empty road for any signs of the other man.

"The Toyota."

"All right. I'm gonna go to his car, the Camaro. I'll wait for him. Jump him from the back seat."

"What should I do?"

Daniel nodded to the other side of the road. "He'll be coming from that side, right?"

"Yeah. The entrance to the driveway is down around the bend," Claire said.

"Good. Then stay here. Keep out of sight."

Claire took a shaky breath. "Okay. All right."

Daniel slid the large kitchen knife out of his belt and looked back at Claire. She stared back with a fragile, frightened look.

"Don't worry. I'll get him. Everything's going to be okay."

Daniel hurried to the Camaro parked behind the Toyota. He

tried the driver's door. Locked. He hobbled over to the passenger door. It was locked too, but the window was open a few inches. Daniel looked around, making sure he was still alone, then reached into the narrow opening. His fingers stretched for the lock. He could almost reach it, but not quite.

He withdrew his hand, considered his options, and tried again, using the knife this time. He slid the blade down to the door lock and started working it back and forth.

Daniel was so intent on his task that he didn't hear the shadowy man with the ax emerge from the bayou behind him. The man hesitated when he saw Daniel at the car. Then he raised the ax and crept closer.

Daniel grimaced and dug the knife deeper under the door lock. It popped up. Daniel sighed, relieved. He was starting to pull his arm out of the narrow window opening when his eyes focused on the glass. In the dirty reflection, Daniel saw the rusty ax rising behind him. At the same instant, Claire screamed to him from her hiding place down the road. "He's behind you!"

Daniel twisted around as the heavy blade swung down into the metal roof with a loud thump, inches from his head. Daniel dropped the knife into the car and tried to pull his arm out of the window in a panic. He wasn't fast enough.

The man grabbed the door and yanked it open, cracking Daniel's arm backward. Daniel cried out in agony. The man kicked Daniel in the stomach, reached for the ax, and tried to free the blade that had lodged in the metal roof. Daniel launched his weight backward, slamming the door into the man. The ax clattered out onto the roadway.

Daniel squirmed around, pulled his arm out of the window, and started for the ax. But the man was already behind the wheel of the Camaro, starting the engine.

Daniel grabbed the ax as the Camaro screeched away,

swerving wildly. Daniel's body glanced off the fender and tumbled to the ground; his head slammed hard against the unforgiving asphalt. He felt a sharp, fiery pain shoot through his skull.

Then everything went black.

FIFTEEN

Daniel was empty.

Alone.

Floating.

There was no telling for how long he had been out when the timeless, deep void began to recede. Daniel struggled to open his eyes. The lacy black pattern of branches in the night sky above him stirred slightly in the warm breeze. The night sounds of the bayou began to fill his ears. He raised his head off the cool asphalt and sat up.

The dark road was deserted.

Daniel looked around. Claire's Toyota was gone. Cliff's body was gone too. There were no bloodstains where Cliff's body had been. No shattered glass from the Toyota's window. No ax. Nothing.

Something else was missing. There was no dull pain throbbing in his calf from the knife wound. He looked down.

There was no blood on his leg.

His knuckles were no longer bloody from being slammed in the door.

"What the fuck?" he whispered as he reached down and pulled up his pant leg. There was a faded scar in his calf where a wound used to be, as though it had happened long ago. Daniel traced his fingers over the faded wound. What new turn had this strange adventure taken now?

Daniel pulled himself to his feet and crossed back to the far side of the road where he had left Claire. She was gone.

"Claire!" his voice echoed into the dark bayou. There was no response. He turned and started down the long bend in the road.

———

Moments later, Daniel was trudging up the dirt driveway. As he rounded the turn, he saw the house through the trees.

And stopped cold.

He hadn't seen the house like this before. It was well painted and kept up. There was a new Honda in the driveway and a well-tended garden beside the barn.

Daniel stared at the strange sight for a moment in silence before continuing up to the front gate. There were no signs of damage or rot anywhere. He pushed through and walked up the nicely paved walkway to the porch. He climbed the steps and paused by the porch swing. There was a Dean Koontz paperback and a newspaper on a wicker table next to a half-finished glass of lemonade. Daniel reached down and picked up the newspaper.

The date on the front page read August 17, 2013. Daniel stared at the date, stunned.

"Can I help you?"

Daniel dropped the newspaper, startled.

Claire was peering at him suspiciously through the screen door.

But it wasn't the same Claire he had known before. Her girlish-pretty face was mature. She had beautiful black hair and graceful, womanly features.

Daniel tried to say something, but no words came to him.

The uncomfortable moment lingered. Claire began to grow worried. The strange man on her porch seemed disoriented. She reached back to close the door; she would call the police and let them deal with it.

"Claire?" Daniel whispered.

Claire hesitated at the sound of her name. She looked back at him. "Do I know you?"

Daniel stepped away from the wicker table and into the porch light. Claire's eyes locked on Daniel's face and a vague memory stirred from somewhere deep inside; she knew this man. There was something familiar about him.

Then it hit her. It was as if the last thirteen years collapsed into thin air. It was he. It was the man who had saved her life that horrible night so long ago.

———

Daniel sat on the couch, struggling to get his bearings as he looked around at the contemporarily decorated living room. Everything was different. He was sitting in the same house he had started to remodel, but there was no evidence of any of his work.

"Here you go."

Daniel looked up and saw Claire come in from the kitchen with two cups of coffee. He reached out and smiled awkwardly. "Thanks."

"Careful. Hot."

He took the cup by the handle and gingerly took a sip of the scalding liquid.

"Sure you don't want anything with it?"

"No, black's perfect. Thanks."

Claire studied the pensive man for a moment. "Are you sure you're all right?"

"No. Yeah. I'm fine. I've just been on the road for so long, I guess I'm a little out of it."

Claire took a seat on the chair opposite the couch. She watched him take another sip. Daniel felt her eyes on him and looked up. They both smiled, easing their way out of the uncomfortable moment.

Claire looked down at her coffee and gave it a few idle stirs with her spoon. "Look I'm sorry. I just don't know what to say," she said. "I mean, I can't tell you how many times I thought about what it would be like to see you again. But now that it's actually happening, it's just so... strange."

"I know what you mean." Daniel felt relieved. He had never been able to put into words what he was feeling, and she was good at it.

"I tried finding you, you know. I just couldn't remember your last name. All I remembered was Daniel."

"Nash. It's Nash."

"Nash. See I don't remember you even saying that."

"There was a lot going on that night. I'm not surprised."

"Yeah."

Daniel took another sip. It was cooling down enough to drink.

"Is the coffee okay?"

"Great. It's great."

Claire leaned back into her chair and sighed a bit anxiously, "So. God, a million questions. I just don't know where to start."

"No hurry." Daniel smiled, and it made her smile too.

"Where'd you come from that night?"

Daniel's smile faded; he would have to be careful now. "Houston. I was just passin' through."

"Yeah, the police said you were probably just passing through. We get a lot of people like that along the highway."

Daniel nodded and relaxed a bit. So far, so good.

"But what about afterward? When the other man drove away? I came out from where you told me to hide and you were gone."

So that was it, Daniel thought. That's when he had slipped into this version of the present. He lowered his coffee cup. "Well," he said, "with that man dead and all, I wasn't sure what to do. I guess I just figured I should get out."

"The police were never after you," Claire said. "I explained everything. They asked who you were, but I couldn't tell them."

"Did they ever find out who the other man was? The one that got away?"

"No. I never got a look at him, really. Did you?"

Daniel shook his head, "Too dark. His face was covered. I did cut him good with the knife across the forearm. He'll have a scar for sure. Did they check hospitals, or anything like that?"

"Never heard." Claire slowly pulled the spoon from her coffee and took a sip. "The guy you shot on the road. He was a local. His name was Cliff Brandt. I didn't really know him. I told the police the other guy was probably someone at the bar that night with him. There were a lot of guys there. I was trying to ignore them."

"So it started at the bar?"

Claire hesitated a moment before answering. It had been a while since she had recounted that night. Even now it was painful., "The Villa. I knew the owner. He used to give me a beer sometimes. Anyway, I guess I had a few too many." She paused, turned her coffee cup in her hands. "I was just listening to music. They started...you know, like guys do...only it got a little too intense." She paused again.

The memory had come back into sharper focus than she thought it would. She could picture the CD jukebox playing. She was leaning over it, looking at the song titles. She took a long swallow of beer. It had started to get warm and bitter. She wanted another one. She heard the guys at the pool table behind her start calling her over. The more she ignored them, the louder they got. First it was innuendo with the pool cue. Then they started in on her ass. Claire made the mistake of tugging down on her shorts self-consciously, but they were too tight and too short to cover up any more of her flesh. Her failed attempt only egged them on. Claire spun around and flipped them off. The entire group began to holler. Claire headed to the bar, weaving on her way. She had lost count of the beers.

"Anyway," she said, breaking out of her reverie, "I left the bar. I was almost home here when my car stalled out. I'd been having trouble with it before. Something about the fuel pump." Claire paused again. She thought back on the frustrated feeling when her car died. She tried restarting it, but the engine just sputtered. She slammed her fist angrily on the wheel and swore. She was about to get out and walk the rest of the way when she saw the headlights approach from behind. "At first I was relieved. It was so dark I didn't really want to walk. Anyway, when I saw it was one of the guys from the bar, I locked the doors and told him to get lost. That only made him madder. He was so drunk. He started rocking the car. I didn't know what to do. Next thing I know, there was this smashing sound, and I looked over. He had broken my wing window with a rock. That's when he got in, and..."

Claire trailed off, swallowed dryly. She took a shaky breath and looked back at Daniel. "You saved my life that night, and I never knew how you got here or why you came. Sometimes it almost seems like a dream."

They sat for a moment in silence. The distance between them seemed to disappear. She managed a painful smile and added softly, "Ever since then, I've been hoping you'd come back, and now here you are."

Daniel's eyes met hers, and everything around him seemed

to vanish. The past. The present. The future. They all seemed to exist at the same time. It was only the two of them, at the center of everything that ever was and everything that would ever be.

Claire looked away; the connection was too intense, and it scared her. "Do you need more coffee?"

Daniel looked down at his cup, uncomfortable too. "No, I'm fine. Thanks."

Claire rose, "Sure? I think I'm going to have some more." She headed off to the kitchen.

Daniel pushed the strange moment out of his thoughts, then got up and strolled after her.

She was pouring some cream into her cup when he stepped into the kitchen door and paused. "So. You work in the area?"

Claire looked up and smiled as she put the cream back in the refrigerator. "Teacher."

"Teacher? Wow, great. What grade?"

"High school. I know, right? I hated high school. Never thought I'd end up teaching it. It's okay, really. I like it enough."

"You ever thought about leaving? I mean, you grew up here, right?"

"I did for a while. After school I was in Baton Rouge. I was married to this guy, a fireman. Didn't work out."

"Sorry to hear that."

"It was for the best, believe me." She took a sip off her new cup, "We were both too young. Nothing about it was quite right. I guess I was always kinda restless. I just felt like I was supposed to be with someone else. You know, it was just this feeling I had." Claire hesitated; she didn't know why she was telling him this, and it sounded silly to her.

But it didn't to Daniel. Their eyes met again, and he smiled warmly.

"Anyway, I moved back here when my mom died and left me

the house." Claire felt she had been revealing too much about herself. "But what about you? You're the mystery man here."

Daniel hesitated before answering. It wasn't that he didn't feel comfortable confiding in her; it was just that he would have to be careful not to tell her too much. The full truth would have to wait until another time. If at all. He shifted in the doorway. "Well, I was married, too, for a while. She passed away from cancer."

"I'm sorry."

"I've sorta just been driftin' around since then."

"And what do you do when you're not saving people?"

"Nothin' too exciting. Construction." Another pause settled in. Daniel took a final drink of his coffee.

This time Claire broke the silence. "Look, I don't know what your plans are. I don't want to keep you if you have some place to be."

"No, actually, I'm okay. I came up this way to see you."

This took Claire back a bit. "Really?"

Daniel's expression froze.

Claire realized how she had sounded, and she added, "I mean, that's great. I'm glad you did."

Daniel set his cup on the counter; maybe this was all too much. He never should have come inside. He cleared his throat. "But I guess I should be goin'." He smiled uncomfortably and started to turn.

Claire felt a sudden panic. Wait. No. Where is he going? The next words out of her mouth surprised even her. "You're welcome to stay if you want."

Daniel stopped. Did she really just say that? He turned back.

Claire felt her face flush. "I mean, if you need a place to stay, there's a guest room off the kitchen here."

And there it was. An invitation. But not just any invitation. Daniel gazed at her and smiled. From the moment he had seen her behind the screen door, he had been overwhelmed by a kind of emotional deja vu. It wasn't just that Claire had become a beautiful woman, it was that she looked at him in a way that made him feel like he was someplace still and serene; a place where he belonged. It was a feeling he hadn't felt in a long time.

There was no other option. Daniel nodded and said, "That would be nice. Thanks."

SIXTEEN

CLAIRE TOOK a deep breath as she stared at herself in the big bathroom mirror. How could this be happening? Her life had been so quiet lately. She had had a difficult couple of years a while ago when her father had died, followed by her mother, but she had been happy to inherit her childhood home. She had settled into her teaching job and had really learned to like it. It was uneventful and predictable. Stable. At the end of each school year, she had treated herself to travel. This year it had been down to Virgin Gorda for two weeks. Snorkeling in The Baths had been her big adventure for the year. She was looking forward to getting back to school and returning to her familiar routine.

But now this. Claire unhooked her bra and tossed it onto the counter. She pulled on her favorite over-sized Saints T-shirt and brushed the hair out of her face. She snapped off the light and passed into her bedroom. There was little left to remind her of what the room looked like when it had been her parents' room so many years ago. When she had moved into it out of the little pink room where she had spent her childhood and high school years, the first thing she had done was completely redecorate the room. It had become her sanctuary. Her safe place.

Claire crossed to her bed and sat on the edge; she tugged the bottom of the T-shirt that was riding up her bare thighs. She was feeling a slight chill. But, she realized, it wasn't a chill. It was something else. It was electric. She felt it all over her body, as though the air were charged with something.

She looked at her closed bedroom door. She was letting a man she barely knew stay the night. What was she thinking?

Claire got up and paced to her door. She reached out to lock the knob, but then she hesitated. Why? A lock wouldn't stop him if he really wanted to come in.

Claire remained frozen at the door. *If he really wanted to come in.* She turned the words over in her mind. Was that what this was all about? She wrapped her arms around herself and rubbed her tingling skin. God, it was as if she were back in high school. It was like the crush she had on Roger Franks.

Claire turned and went back to her bed. She pulled her covers aside and slid underneath. She settled back into the pillow and took another slow, deep breath. A new feeling crept over her. It was a clear, certain feeling: whatever had made her invite him to stay was certainly going to change her life.

———

Daniel lay awake on the narrow bed in the darkness. His eyes wandered through the small guest room; it didn't look all that different from the version he had stayed in before. Cleaner and more kept up, but not much different. His door was left open a just a bit. A night light from the kitchen filtered in.

Claire was right upstairs. All alone.

Daniel took a shallow breath, exhaled long and slow. It was going to be a long night, and just in case, his door would be open for her the entire time.

———

An ear-splitting explosion shook the old house to its foundation. Daniel's eyes snapped open. KABOOM! The house rattled again.

Daniel leaped out of bed and raced out across the kitchen. He scanned the living room in a blind panic. What the fuck was this? After everything he'd been through, this could be almost anything.

Once more, the house rocked with a deep, thundering crash. It was coming from upstairs. Daniel ran to the staircase and bounded upstairs into the hall. A cloud of dust and debris billowed toward him. KABASH! A sledgehammer exploded through the wall at the end of the hall next to Claire's childhood room.

Daniel raced through the dusty grit, holding his breath and squinting. He reached the doorway and stopped cold.

It was Reggie Waters.

Reggie saw Daniel and checked his swing with the sledgehammer. "Oh, dude. Were you sleepin'? Claire didn't tell me anyone else was here." Reggie yanked off his dust mask and smiled at Daniel.

Daniel took a moment to absorb the young man. There was something different about him; he was better groomed and more muscular than the version of himself in the alternative time line. Daniel realized he was staring, and his attention snapped back to the events at hand. "What's going on?"

Reggie shrugged and wiped his mouth on his sleeve. "Just doin' my job."

Claire appeared behind Daniel. "Oh, I'm so sorry," she said. "I should've told you that Reggie was going to be starting early."

Daniel turned to her; she was dressed in jeans and a blouse. She was radiant and bright and looked like she had been up for hours.

"Why is he tearing this wall down?"

"It's part of my remodel. I've been saving up for a few years to do it."

Daniel soaked in her warm smile.

She was oblivious. Completely unaware of the potential hazard she was facing, that they *all* were facing if she allowed Reggie to continue removing walls.

Daniel took her arm and pulled her aside in the hall. "Claire, listen to me. Removing walls in an old house like this can change the flow of energy. There's a history that's built up over time, a stored energy. When you start moving things around, it can change everything."

Claire's smile faded on her face when she saw him looking at her so intently. "I've got a permit," she offered innocently.

At that moment, Daniel could see how vast the void was between what he knew and what he could tell her. He eased off. "Look, I know it probably sounds a little nuts, but..."

"Dude, there's nothin' to worry about, really," said Reggie, who had joined them in the hall. "I brought a structural engineer in here. We're not taking out any load-bearing walls. Promise."

Daniel looked over at Reggie. Now there were two of them looking at him, concerned.

A smile slowly returned to Claire's face, "Reggie's really a great contractor. He knows what he's doing. I hired him a couple years ago to rebuild the barn."

"She gave me my start," Reggie joined in proudly. "Been working solid ever since. Three years now."

"Daniel's a contractor, too," Claire explained to Reggie.

There was no way Daniel could begin to explain. It wasn't going to do any good to warn them about something that was unconnected to anything they were aware of. Daniel painted on a smile. "Yeah, look, I'm sorry. I didn't mean to cause any trouble about all this."

"No sweat, dude," Reggie smiled back.

"I just had a bad experience once during a remodel, that's all."

"Yeah, a couple of my first jobs were kinda rough too. You get past it." Reggie pulled his mask back up over his nose and mouth. "You guys will probably wanna head on outta here." He grabbed the sledgehammer and hefted it over his shoulder.

Daniel watched him disappear into the room.

"You coming?"

Daniel looked over at Claire, who was already halfway down the hall.

"Yeah, yeah." Daniel caught up with her.

"So. You decide what you're gonna do?

"No, not really. Hadn't given it much thought yet."

"Well I've got to go into town and pick up some stuff for work. If you wanna come along, we can grab some breakfast."

"That would be great. Lemme get my shirt and shoes."

Daniel had jumped out of bed so fast he was still wearing only his jeans. He was lucky he hadn't stepped on something and hurt himself.

Downstairs in the guest room, he plucked his shirt from the end of the small bed and pulled it on. He went into the small bathroom and snapped on the light. Shit. He looked like hell. He ran his fingers through his hair, doing his best to push the tangled blonde mess into some kind of shape, then cranked on the faucet in the little sink and splashed his face. He would have to take a shower when he got back.

Daniel rubbed the water from his eyes and shut off the faucet. He reached over for the small towel, and his eyes wandered back to the dingy mirror.

A man was standing in the door behind him.

Daniel spun around, startled. "Shit!"

The steely-eyed man stared back at him, unblinking; he looked to be in his mid 30s and had a coarse, hard-edged feel about him. His face was pock-marked from some kind of severe childhood skin condition. "Reggie around?" he asked.

Daniel took a moment to catch his breath. "Reggie?"

"Yeah. He around?"

"Upstairs."

Claire called from the other room, "Daniel? You ready?"

Daniel eyed the man a moment longer. "Excuse me." He pushed past the man, who barely moved to get out of his way.

Claire approached from across the kitchen, and Daniel joined her. He shot a look back at the odd man as he followed them out.

Claire grabbed her car keys off the table, smiled at the man. "Oh, hi," she said. "You're working with Reggie, right? I'm Claire."

"Nick."

"Reggie's upstairs."

"Yeah. Yeah, I told him," Daniel said.

They started out the door as the man crossed to the staircase.

As Daniel followed Claire out the door, he couldn't help but take another look at the man. It was strange how relaxed and trusting Claire seemed with a stranger in her house. Especially this one. For Daniel, it was only the night before when he and Claire were fighting for their lives. For Claire, it was over a decade ago. She had earned her right to let her guard down. But not Daniel. Daniel couldn't help feeling suspicious. There was something about the pock-marked man that put him off.

———

The main street of Krotz Springs looked remarkably similar to the one Daniel had first encountered: same worn-out sidewalks and rusting buildings. Claire pulled her Honda up to the Krotz Diner and parked. Daniel hesitated as he climbed out. He looked more carefully at the street, trying to orient himself; things weren't the same after all.

"Didn't this used to be a butcher shop?"

Claire gave him an odd look. The diner had, in fact, been the butcher shop when she had been growing up. "So weird you'd mention that," she said.

"Is it?"

She paused at the diner door and turned back. "It belonged to the Brandts."

It was clear from the look on Daniel's face that he had no idea why this would be weird. "Cliff Brandt's parents," she said. "They moved out of town after you...I mean, after Cliff was..." Claire trailed off, not sure exactly how to finish what she had started.

Of course. Daniel realized he had to be more careful with what he said. Now she was feeling awkward. "Right, right. Yeah," he muttered.

Daniel ended the strained moment by pushing open the door and gesturing for her to go inside. It was strangely similar to the décor from when it had been a butcher shop. It had the same linoleum floor and high-gloss white walls. Even the overhead lights were the same. Of course, it hadn't been that long since Daniel had seen what this place had looked like more than a decade ago.

Daniel followed Claire down the narrow room and glanced at the door to the small office in the back, where he had found the article about her murder.

"Here okay?"

Daniel looked at Claire, who was gesturing to a booth. "Yeah, great."

She slid into the booth opposite him, and he was taking the seat across when another thought crept over him. The man in the back of the butcher shop with Cliff that day. The lunatic that was skull-fucking the severed pig's head. Had they ever questioned that man about that night? They were about the same age. It was a small town. Could he and Cliff have been friends that long ago?

Daniel's mind began to race with the possibility. His name tag. Alex. That was it. Alex. He could've been the one with Cliff that night. The one who got away.

"Coffee?"

"Huh?" Daniel looked up and saw the elderly waitress holding a pot. Claire already had a full cup and menus in front of her. "Oh, yeah. That would be great."

The waitress poured the coffee. Daniel looked over at Claire, who was perusing the menu. He opened his mouth to say something but stopped himself. She was already beginning to sense something was off with him. How could he start asking her about Cliff's friend Alex? How would he be able to tell her he even knew Alex had been Cliff's co-worker at the butcher shop? Maybe he had worked there when Daniel had visited the butcher shop, but he hadn't worked there before that. So maybe he had been friends with Cliff only in the other time line. Shit, this was getting too confusing. Daniel's head began to hurt.

He picked up the menu and glanced down at the breakfast offerings. He would not say anything to Claire about Alex, or about his suspicions of Nick. He'd give himself some time to think things out, then he could start doing his own investigation to find out who the other man was that night.

———

Twenty minutes later, Claire was looking at Daniel over a cup of coffee as they ate their breakfast. "I don't know how you do it," she said, "just move around all the time. I like being in one place. Of course, I guess that's pretty obvious. I'm still living in the house I grew up in."

"I didn't always move around a lot. I was in Houston for a long time when I was married." Daniel paused for a sip of orange juice.

"I guess I haven't found a reason to stay in one place since then, that's all."

Daniel smiled and was more than happy when she smiled back at him. She knew what he was saying. He took another bite of his omelet, and she sipped more coffee. "You think Reggie could use some help with your remodel?"

Claire hesitated before taking a bite of her toast. "I don't know. We could ask him."

This time, the smile lingered between them. Claire looked away. Everything was moving so fast, and yet it was so effortless, as though it was supposed to be like this.

"That your Honda out front, Claire?" A deep voice interrupted. They both looked up.

It was Officer Bleeker, standing beside their booth. Claire straightened in her seat. "Yeah, Arnie. It's mine."

A smile curled up on Bleeker's face. "Thought so. Time's expired. I put a quarter in there for you."

Daniel couldn't help but notice how odd a friendly smile looked on the beefy man's square face. Even his thick black eyebrows seemed to sit lightly on his forehead.

Claire shifted her gaze back to Daniel, who looked back down at his orange juice and took a sip. "Thanks, Arnie," she said, still looking at Daniel.

Bleeker shot a look back and forth between Daniel and Claire. It was as if he had caught them at something. "Getting' ready to go back to school soon?" he asked.

"Next week," Claire said.

"You make our alma mater proud, huh?"

"I always try."

Bleeker looked back at Daniel. An awkward silence set in. Claire noticed, and said, "This is Daniel."

Daniel shot Bleeker a cursory nod. "Hey."

Claire continued, "Daniel's the man who..."

"Came down from Houston to help her remodel." Daniel finished her words.

Claire gave Daniel another odd look. Was he worried she would tell Bleeker that he was the one who shot Cliff all those years ago? Of course, that wasn't what she was going to say, but it seemed that Daniel thought she would bring up the past in front of the policeman.

"Houston, huh? I took down a couple license plates from Texas just yesterday," said Bleeker. "We get a lotta people drifting through. I like to keep an eye on things."

"Of course you do." Daniel couldn't help an ironic tone slipping into his response. This might be an alternate time, but some people were the same in any time line.

"Say what?"

"Huh? Oh, nothin'," Daniel mumbled, as he took another sip of his juice.

Bleeker focused more closely on the stranger. Right off the bat, he had two strikes against him: One, he was from out of town, and two, he was with Claire.

Bleeker had known Claire her entire life and had never given up the idea that maybe, one day, she and he would get together. But it had never happened. Here he was, married to another woman, two kids, the whole thing, but every time he saw her he couldn't help it. He used to freeze up around her when he was younger, and he had pined away sleepless nights thinking about what it would be like to be with her. Every detail of her. She was his one and only original crush.

Bleeker smiled once more at her. "Don't let those meters get you, Claire."

"I'll watch them. Thanks, Arnie."

Bleeker moved toward the cashier, and Daniel watched him pay for his breakfast.

"You and he grow up together?"

"We went to the same schools."

Daniel looked back at Bleeker. The thick man shot a look back. Their eyes locked. The moment seemed to stretch a bit too long, then Bleeker looked away and went out the door.

"Something wrong?"

Daniel looked back at Claire, a bit shaken. Yes. There was something... But what? There was no way Bleeker could possibly remember him, could there be? Daniel had been in another time line when they met. Still, something was off, and Daniel wasn't sure what it could be.

He took another sip of coffee and pushed the thought aside. He was going to have to get used to feelings like this.

"Naw," he answered Claire. "Nothin'. Nothin'."

—————

Bleeker stepped out the door and paused. Jesus fucking Christ, could it be? He peered back through the diner, trying to get another look at Daniel, but the glare was too strong. He looked away and started slowly back to his cruiser as his mind raced.

The sound of rattling bikes grabbed Bleeker's attention, and he looked over. Two local boys were cruising past on the street. "Hey, Arnie!"

Bleeker smiled paternally. "You boys heading down to swim?"

"You bet!"

"Good day for it. Looks like it's gonna be another cooker."

The boys waved over their shoulders as they sped on their way. Bleeker threw open the cruiser door and slid behind the wheel. He hesitated again and squinted over at the diner.

Now he was sure. Daniel's was definitely a face he knew.

—————

The food had been much better than Daniel had expected. Of course there was no shortage of butter and bacon fat, and that always helped. Claire had gone to use the restroom, and Daniel was at the register, paying the tab. The elderly waitress smiled as she counted out the change. He thanked her and pushed out the door.

Daniel stood outside the diner and looked up and down the main drag, taking a closer look at the familiar street. Was there anything else that had changed in this time line after he killed Cliff? Was it only the butcher shop? Was the so-called "Butterfly Effect" really just a fanciful notion, and even changes as big as saving lives and killing others in the past didn't have any global effect?

Looking at the street now, Daniel got the sense that people's lives weren't as significant in the larger world as they would like to think. Things were scaled much smaller than that. Even things like…

Angie.

If Cho was right, then everything that had happened before he created the change was still the same. His life with Angie. Her painful ending. If only he had been able to go back and do for her what he had done for Claire.

A pang of guilt rose in Daniel. It had been days since he had thought of Angie. He had spent all his time with her on his mind, and now it was different. There was Claire.

Daniel took an anxious breath. Damn, this was going to take some getting used to. The door to the diner behind him opened.

Daniel turned and saw Claire stepping out with a warm smile on her face. "Well? You like it?"

"It was great," Daniel smiled back.

"Thanks. Next time it's on me."

They started to her car, and all of Daniel's anxiety disappeared. This was right. Everything about the two of them was the way it should be.

Claire slid behind the wheel and started the engine. Daniel opened the passenger door and got in too.

———

As they pulled away from the diner, neither one of them noticed the man who was watching them from the diner as he bussed their dishes. He had kept his eye on them the whole time he had made their breakfast. He couldn't help it; there was something off about the new guy. It wasn't just that he was a stranger. It was that he was with Claire.

As it pulled away, the Honda disappeared from his sight through the diner windows, and the order bell dinged loudly.

"Alex! Set up a four top in back, would you?"

Alex looked at the busy waitress as she served a hungry customer his plate of biscuits and gravy.

"Yeah. Got it," he said, as he finished wiping down the Formica tabletop. As he passed the kitchen, he couldn't help but remember what the place looked like when he had worked in the butcher shop with Cliff all those years ago.

SEVENTEEN

AT THE END of the day, Daniel followed Reggie out to his new Ford. Reggie had agreed to bring Daniel on, and he would start the following morning. As Daniel helped Reggie put his tools away, he smiled to himself. It was ironic that he was going to be working for Reggie. Saving Claire had led to her giving Reggie his first break as a contractor, and Reggie had risen to the occasion. At least this was some evidence of the Butterfly Effect.

Then Daniel shot a look over at Nick, the man who had startled him this morning.

Daniel still couldn't get a bead on this guy, and it bothered him. Daniel had flip-flopped all day long on his opinion. Was Nick just a quiet type? Or was he holding back something? It was easy for Daniel to be suspicious. Nick fit the bill physically when it came to matching the man who had gotten away. Daniel had tried to get a look for any signs of old scars on his arm, but the guy kept his sleeves pulled down, which was strange because it was so warm.

Daniel sighed anxiously. Damn, he had every right to be paranoid, didn't he? Or did he? If he were going to settle in this time line, he'd have to find a way to let the past go. Whoever had gotten away that night could be long gone by now. Maybe even dead. There was no way of telling.

"Tomorrow, then."

Daniel looked over and saw Reggie extending his hand. "Huh? Oh, yeah. Definitely." Daniel shook Reggie's hand.

"Give you a lift somewhere?"

Daniel hesitated and looked back at the house. "No thanks. I'm gonna hang here for a bit."

Reggie's smile became a warm little laugh as he climbed into his truck. Nick was in the passenger seat. "Be good to her," Reggie said. "She's a sweet woman. Did me a real favor getting me started in business and all."

"Yeah."

Reggie started up the engine and dropped it into gear, "See you in the morning. We start at—"

"Seven sharp. Yeah, I know."

Reggie pulled out and waved. Nick stared straight forward. Daniel watched them disappear down the driveway, then turned and started into the house.

Claire was busy packing up photographs from the fireplace mantle when Daniel came inside. He paused a moment, watching her as she worked. She felt his presence and looked around, smiling. "Hey."

"Can I give you a hand with that?"

"Sure. Reggie said you guys are gonna start work in here tomorrow. He wants everything out."

Daniel came over and started helping her take down the pictures. "Any particular order?"

"No. Just the big ones on the bottom." Claire picked up a picture of her as a little girl on the front porch and hesitated. "I know the house is gonna look much better with the remodel..., but it was hard at first. I had a good life growing up here. Part of me wants to keep everything the same."

Daniel picked up one of Claire's teen-age pictures. She looked over and smiled, embarrassed, "Ugh. Except that. That's gonna stay in a box."

"Oh come on, you were beautiful." Daniel hesitated, then smiled. "Well, cute anyway." He looked more closely at the picture. "This is about what you looked like the last time I saw you."

"Yeah, I think you're right. It was the summer after I graduated."

"You were around eighteen?"

"Yeah. God, it's amazing, all the stupid things I did. I never should've been drinking at that age."

"Wouldn't be the first teenager."

Claire gazed pensively at herself from ten years ago. "You know, sometimes I can't help but wonder what would've happened to me if you hadn't been here that night. Everything you did, for someone you didn't even know."

"It never seemed that way to me."

"What didn't?"

"That I didn't know you."

Daniel looked up at her and their eyes met. They were close now, inches apart. There was a quiet, connected moment, then Claire spoke softly. "I'm glad you came back."

"I am, too."

Claire reached out and ran her fingers gently down his rugged cheek. Daniel leaned in and kissed her, long and deep. Claire was instantly lost, and she pulled him close against her. Their kisses grew hotter, their breath shorter. Daniel eased them away from the fireplace, and they collapsed onto the couch. Their bodies found each other. Claire pulled back, catching her breath, then started clawing at Daniel's T-shirt. It was off in an instant. Her blouse came off next, then her jeans. Daniel's followed. Nothing could stop this now. It wasn't them. It was something much bigger. It was inevitable. They had both known it the moment they had seen each other.

And now it was real.

———

Daniel slept deeply in Claire's arms. It was a serenity he hadn't felt in a long time. There was none of his usual restlessness, or the feeling that he had someplace else to be. Everything felt just right.

But then, for no apparent reason his eyes snapped open.

It was late. The house was quiet. He looked over at Claire, naked next to him on the couch. He slipped his arm out from under her and sat up.

What had awoken him? He took a moment to orient himself; it wasn't anything he could put his finger on. The now-familiar night sounds of the bayou filtered in from outside; a frog croaked rhythmically. Then it hit him-

The room was completely dark; there was no yellow light coming in from the porch.

He got up and crossed to the kitchen. The clock on the stove was out. He reached over and tried the switch. Nothing. It was dead.

He crossed to the front door and tried the light switch just for the hell of it, and of course nothing happened. He unlocked the front door and opened it.

The late night air was cooler than he had ever felt it before as he crossed to the edge of the porch. The frog croaked steadily against the soft chirp of crickets. He paused, scanning the shadowy yard. It was probably a downed transformer somewhere.

He would have to find the central circuit breaker to the house just to make sure.

The porch creaked behind him.

Daniel spun around, startled. It was Claire.

"What's going on?" she asked.

Daniel looked back out into the darkness. "I don't know. The power's off to the entire house. Does that happen a lot out here?"

"Not that much." Claire tugged on the bottom of her oversized Saints shirt; she could sense Daniel's growing unease. "What are you looking for?"

"I don't know. It's just..." his voice trailed away. Something was off. Maybe it was all the times he had spent here at night when things had gone so horribly wrong. Or maybe it was something real. In the end, it didn't matter. He had a bad feeling, and he wasn't going to ignore it. "Get back inside."

"You're scaring me."

"Just do it."

Claire turned and went back to the front door. Daniel lingered for a moment, keeping his eye on the dark yard, then turned.

BOOM. A gunshot flashed from the darkness. Claire spun back around and screamed. "Daniel!"

Daniel felt a searing throb in his shoulder as he reeled back. He looked down and saw blood oozing through his shirt. "Inside! Get inside!"

Claire pulled Daniel through the door, and they slammed it tight. The pain burned, and Daniel clutched his arm. "Lock it!"

Claire threw the deadbolt and returned to Daniel. He pulled her next to him. "Stay down!" he whispered.

They ducked behind the couch. Daniel tested his wound gingerly. "It's okay. It didn't hit me straight on."

"What is all this? Who's out there?" Claire gasped.

"I don't know." Daniel winced. "I didn't see anyone." He

pressed his hand against the graze. "Stay here." He got up, crept to the front window, pressed against the wall, and pulled the cord to the curtains until they were shut tight. He took a moment to catch his breath, then hurried to the telephone by the stairs and snatched it up.

Silence. The phone was dead.

"Cell phone?"

"In my car."

"Your car?"

"I always forget to take it to work with me, so I keep it in there."

"Perfect." Daniel hung up the house phone, his mind racing. "This is all connected."

"What is?"

"This. All this. I showed my face around town with you today." He looked over at Claire, who remained crouched behind the couch. "Whoever got away that night must have recognized me and has come back to cover his tracks." Daniel winced again, checked his shoulder, and started over to the kitchen.

"Wait." Claire hopped up and hurried after him.

Daniel hurried to the back door and twisted the lock. He grabbed a dishtowel, folded it, and tucked it under his sleeve against his wound. "You have a gun in the house?"

"No guns."

Daniel pulled open the familiar knife drawer. It was full of silverware. "Where're the knives? There used to be knives in here."

Claire gave him another odd look. "Not for years," she said. She pulled open another drawer and took out a couple of large knives. "Here."

Daniel took the knife. "Flashlight?"

Claire went to the refrigerator, pulled a magnetic flashlight off of it, and clicked it on.

"There's no other way into the house, is there?"

"Just the cellar. There's an outside door to the cellar."

Daniel looked at the narrow door in the laundry room off the kitchen. "Does that door go down to the cellar?"

"Yeah."

Daniel went to the door, pulled it open, and shined the flashlight down the narrow old steps. Claire came up behind him. "Let's just try to get to my car," she said.

"It's at least ten yards to your car in the open. He'd pick us off easy. We're better off defending ourselves from the house."

Daniel looked back across the kitchen and thought about the house; there were too many windows and doors to defend. They'd never be able to cover all of them. He looked back at Claire. "All right. We hole up down there."

"The cellar?"

"It's our best bet. Only two doors to defend."

Claire sighed anxiously and looked down the cellar steps.

Daniel placed his hand on her arm reassuringly. "It's almost four a.m. Reggie will be here at seven," he said. "We can do this."

Reggie, he thought. Nick had driven away with Reggie. Had he begged a ride just so far, then gone to where he had a gun stashed in the woods and come back? Daniel had never been able to get a glimpse of the strange man's arm, to see if he had a scar. Was he way off with his suspicions of Nick? He must be. It had been the trip into town that had lured their attacker here. Someone had seen them at the diner, or driving down the main street.

Daniel grabbed a china plate from the cabinet, stepped through the door, and pulled Claire in behind him. He closed the cellar door tight and leaned the plate up against it. They'd hear it fall if the door was opened.

Daniel turned and started down the rickety steps, with Claire close behind him. They reached the bottom and paused. Daniel panned the flashlight through the shadowy maze of cobweb-covered junk: rusted bikes, wagons and toys. Stacks of dusty boxes. Old luggage.

"Where's the cellar door?" he asked.

"On the other side. Behind the furnace."

Daniel started in the direction Claire was pointing. A low creak and a dull bump came from the shadows beyond. Daniel snapped off the flashlight.

"What?" she asked.

Daniel held up his hand, silencing her. They waited in the darkness for a moment, listening. Then Daniel continued forward with his knife poised, ready to strike. They moved around the large, old oil furnace, and the cellar door came into view.

It was open and creaking back and forth in a slight breeze.

Daniel faded back behind the furnace and whispered urgently to Claire. "Is it always open like that?"

"I'm not sure. I haven't been down here in a long time."

Daniel scanned the surrounding shadows and clutter and braced himself. He stepped back around the furnace and sneaked toward the cellar door, keeping his eye on potential hiding places along the way. He reached out. His hand grabbed the cellar door.

A shadow passed by outside the dingy casement window.

"Daniel!" Claire whispered hoarsely as she pointed at the window.

Daniel looked over at her, startled.

WHAP! A hand grabbed the outside of the cellar door and yanked it open. The intruder's other hand jammed a pistol into the opening. BOOM!

It was a wild shot. Daniel yanked back on the door, crushing the intruder's wrist. A painful groan came from the other side of the door. Daniel kicked the pistol out of the wounded hand. The pistol fired wildly as it hit the floor. The bullet thwacked the jamb. The unseen intruder let the door go and it slammed shut.

Daniel grabbed the pistol, scrambled back behind the furnace and took aim at the casement window. Footsteps could be heard retreating. Daniel held his shot.

Shit. He had done it. He had managed to disarm the guy. Daniel checked the chamber. Four bullets left. Of course it was possible the intruder had another gun, but at least things were more even now.

"We should try to get to your car now. We can cover ourselves with this," he said. He clicked the chamber closed. "We'll go out the front. It's the shortest distance." Daniel took Claire's hand and led the way back across the cellar. They crept up the stairs. Daniel reached the top, moved the plate out of the way, and pushed open the door.

The kitchen was dark. Quiet. He stepped out, scanning the shadowy house. It was empty. Daniel signaled Claire, and she stepped out behind him.

They crept across the kitchen and into the living room. They were almost to the front door.

A rocking chair from the front porch exploded through the front window in a shower of glass. It slammed into Daniel, knocking him to the floor. Claire screamed and ran to the stairs.

The intruder leaped in the window and tackled Daniel. Daniel smashed his open palm into the intruder's neck. The intruder cried out and reeled back into a pool of moonlight. Daniel looked up.

It was Bleeker. Not Nick at all. Not someone who had seen them in town. Bleeker.

Bleeker saw the startled look on Daniel's face and seized the opportunity. He scrambled over and grabbed the loose pistol. But before he could stand, he felt Daniel's heavy body slam into his back. With a surge of adrenaline, Bleeker sprung back, smashing Daniel against the wall with the entire weight of his thick body. He could hear Daniel's ribs crack.

Daniel groaned and collapsed, landing hard on the floor. Bleeker reeled around, catching his breath. He gave Daniel a solid kick in the torso. Daniel's limp body slumped back. There was no sound.

Daniel was out cold.

EIGHTEEN

Through the years, Bleeker had managed to put the memory of that dark night at The Villa into a small corner of his mind. The more time passed, the more distant and unreal it all seemed. It wasn't until he got a look at Daniel at the diner that everything started to creep back up on him.

It had been a hot, sticky night fueled by liquor and lust. He and Cliff watched Claire from across the bar as she teased the guys at the pool table. He boiled when he saw how flirtatious she was; all the years of pining away for her, and here she was, begging to be taken. The more she drank, the more Bleeker burned up inside, and his own drinking began to outpace even hers. There wasn't anyone in The Villa who didn't know what she wanted.

When Claire staggered out, Cliff and he followed her "to make sure she got home okay."

As they followed Claire's car, Bleeker struggled to stay awake, but eventually the alcohol caught up with him. He ended up passing out in Cliff's Camaro and woke only when he heard the sound of breaking glass; he looked up and saw Cliff chasing Claire off into the swamp. He tried to follow, but he lost them in the darkness and ended up going to Claire's house.

The rest of that night had only gone from bad to worse, and the next morning he waited for the shit to hit the fan. But it never did. That's when he knew for sure that Claire had never seen who was in the Camaro that night.

Eventually, Bleeker just locked away all the events of that night and pretended it had never happened. When Claire had returned to Krotz Springs after college, he began to get along pretty well with her, and his old crush re-surfaced.

Until this morning.

Bleeker had spent the whole day agonizing over his next move once he had seen Daniel. He replayed the moments at the diner over and over, trying to decide if Daniel had recognized him. What made the stranger come back? Had Claire found him? Did he come on his own? If so, why now?

Then there was that final look Daniel gave him when he was leaving. If it wasn't a look of recognition, it was a look that said something had seemed familiar, and even though Bleeker had been careful to cover his face all those years ago, they had been close that night when they fought, and it was possible Daniel had seen his face.

In the end, it all came down to loose ends. It's never good to have loose ends, especially loose ends that could destroy your life.

Once he had made the decision, the solutions came easy for Bleeker. After all, Daniel was just a drifter from Texas, and drifters come and go.

This one would just have to go.

That left Claire. As hard as it would have to be, it was time to put childish dreams behind him. She would never have him. She could only ruin him. He would make it look like the drifter killed her.

———

Bleeker stood over Daniel's unconscious body as he considered his next move. He had to stage this the right way. The angle of the shot and the placement of Daniel's body had to look like Daniel had killed Claire before Bleeker shot him. He would have to stage Claire's body after he shot Daniel. Not ideal. It was a lot to figure out in a short time.

The old ceiling creaked above him. Bleeker looked up. Claire was up there. There were also a number of windows she could climb out if she was desperate enough. Shit.

Desperate enough? Of course she was desperate enough. He'd have to deal with Daniel after he had taken care of Claire.

Bleeker darted over to the staircase.

Upstairs, Claire could hear Bleeker's heavy boots coming up the stairs. She stumbled down the hall and ducked through the partially opened wall and into her childhood room. She pressed into the shadows by the door and raised her knife.

Bleeker's footsteps pounded to the head of the stairs and stopped. Claire tensed and stopped breathing. His footsteps thumped down the hall, growing louder. She saw his shadow pass by the partially open wall and disappear again. She turned, leaving her back to the open wall as she followed the sound of his footsteps. They neared the doorway and stopped.

Claire's eyes were locked on the doorway. There was silence. Claire remained frozen. A moment passed. Then another. Why wasn't he coming through the door?

Claire leaned closer to the door, raising her knife, ready to strike.

She never saw the pistol barrel push through the open wall behind her and aim at the back of her head.

Downstairs, Daniel stirred groggily. His eyes fluttered open, and the world came back into focus. Then he remembered. He inhaled and felt the stabbing pain from his cracked ribs. He looked around. No Bleeker. No Claire. This wasn't good. Daniel grimaced and sat up. He pushed through the stabbing pain in his ribs and staggered to his feet.

Upstairs, the pistol barrel stopped inches from the back of Claire's head as she stared at the dark doorway. Then she sensed something behind her.

She spun.

BOOM!

The bullet ripped past her head. She screamed and lashed out at Bleeker with her knife. The blade grazed his hand. He bellowed in agony and burst through the open wall. He swung his heavy boot into her torso. She was propelled across the room and crashed brutally against the wall. Bleeker staggered toward her. She looked up at him looming above her. Her mouth went dry, and sheer terror left her paralyzed. "Please. Please, no," she begged.

Bleeker pulled back the hammer, leveling the barrel at her head.

Daniel reeled into the doorway behind them as Bleeker pulled the trigger.

And Claire was dead.

NINETEEN

Daniel screamed out in horror and charged Bleeker in a blind rage. Bleeker reeled around as Daniel smashed into him. They both crashed into the construction rubble. Bleeker slammed to the floor, losing his grip on the pistol.

Daniel felt the whole world telescope into blackness. No more pain. He saw nothing except Bleeker. He leaped on top of the husky man and began pummeling his face. Blood sprayed up from Bleeker's broken nose and Daniel's raw knuckles. Daniel didn't stop. He was completely lost now. There was nothing except his singular desire to destroy the monster who had just taken every-thing from him.

It was time to kill.

Over and over, Daniel pounded the bloody face. Past. Present. Future. It all stood still, until Daniel felt his hands aching from the effort. He looked away from the bloody man's face. Now he would put a bullet into his hellish head and finish him off.

But when Daniel looked for the pistol, it was gone.

Daniel scanned the rubble. Nothing. No pistol.

He turned to Claire.

Claire's body was gone, too.

All that was left in the room were Daniel and Bleeker.

What the fuck?

BOOM! A gunshot echoed from outside the front of the house. Daniel heard Claire scream his name. He looked out the window and saw a man.

Himself.

On the front porch.

Jesus Christ. It was happening. He had slipped back in time again. But how? Why now?

Claire, Daniel decided. It had to be Claire.

She had been the only thing holding him to the time line, and now that she had been killed, he had drifted again. Only this time, he was clutching Bleeker, so they had both slipped together. But they hadn't slipped back far. Judging from what he was seeing out the window now, it was only about ten minutes earlier.

Daniel watched, stunned, as he saw Claire help him back inside as he clutched his wounded arm. Just as he had done before.

WHAP! Bleeker's beefy hand slapped itself around Daniel's neck. Daniel recoiled. Bleeker's beaten and bloody face was looking at the window below, equally as puzzled.

"What the fuck is going on?" Bleeker gurgled.

"Same shit. Two different times," Daniel gasped as he clawed at Bleeker's hands around his throat.

But Bleeker wasn't looking at Daniel. Bleeker's attention remained transfixed on the window. He watched as he saw himself from ten minutes ago heading around the house to the cellar door.

None of this made sense to Bleeker. How could that be him? "Wh... who...?" he stammered. Bleeker shoved Daniel away and staggered to the door and into the hall. He tried to wipe away the blood that was streaming into his eyes, but the flow was too great. He was disoriented, dazed, and lost.

Daniel grabbed a two-by-four from the rubble and bolted out behind him. Bleeker was nearing the door to the master bedroom when Daniel swung hard and smashed him in the back of the head.

The beefy man crashed into the bedroom. Daniel came in and loomed over him, brandishing the heavy wood. Bleeker looked up at him, a bewildered expression on his bloody and broken face.

Daniel glared down at him; there was no hint of sympathy for the confused man. The second gunshot rang out from down in the cellar. They heard the cellar door slam shut and heard Bleeker from ten minutes ago running away.

Bleeker looked back at Daniel. "How? How is this happen...?"

Daniel raised the two-by-four high above the man. He hesitated, and he even considered telling the horrible man the truth before sending him to his grave.

But the thought lasted only a split second. No. Let him die in purgatory.

Daniel brought the two-by-four down onto Bleeker's skull with all his might.

Bleeker died hearing the sickening crack of bone and cartilage of his own skull, as the two-by-four shattered its way into his brain.

Daniel stood back, dropped the two-by-four, and caught his breath. The stabbing pain from his ribs started moving back through his chest.

The sound of the earlier Bleeker hurling the porch chair through the living room window came from downstairs. Daniel spun around and heard Claire's scream. He heard the earlier version of himself struggling with Bleeker. Seconds later, Claire's footsteps pounded up the stairs. Daniel looked out the bedroom door and began to see everything that had happened up here while he had been incapacitated downstairs ten minutes ago.

Daniel started to call after Claire but stopped himself when he heard Bleeker's footsteps coming up the staircase. Daniel faded back into the shadows.

Bleeker raced into the hall, paused, and listened, as he had before. He heard a noise from the corner room and crept toward it with his pistol poised.

Daniel stepped into the hall behind Bleeker. He could do this. He could kill Bleeker before he shot Claire.

Outside the pink room, Bleeker slipped up to the open wall and started to push the barrel toward the back of Claire's head, as before.

But this time, things changed.

Daniel leaped up behind Bleeker and tackled him. The pistol fired wildly. Claire screamed and retreated deeper into the room.

Bleeker reeled around and body-slammed Daniel. The two men launched backward.

The upstairs window of the old house exploded into the misty night air. Daniel and Bleeker's bodies sailed outward in a shower of glass, then plummeted down together, tumbling through the darkness. Time stretched into slow motion. Daniel fought to separate himself from Bleeker. The stocky man clung tightly until the last moment, when his hands slipped free. Their bodies separated by inches. The last things Bleeker saw were the pointed pickets of the wrought-iron fence rushing toward him from below.

CRACK! Bleeker's beefy body impaled itself on the iron pickets.

Daniel tumbled past him, just missing the fence. He rolled to a stop in the yard.

Blackness consumed Daniel once more.

———

The bayou sounds drifted back to Daniel from the distance. He opened his eyes and gazed up at the unfocused maze of shadowy branches above him. He inhaled. His ribs no longer hurt. His vision focused itself, and he began to have a familiar feeling. It was the same feeling he had when he had woken up on the roadway. He was rooted again. He was completely stuck in one time line again.

But which one? Daniel grimaced, sat up, and oriented himself.

Bleeker's body was next to him, impaled on the fence. The window was blown open above. This was a good sign. Very good. This was the time line in which he had just saved Claire upstairs.

Daniel climbed to his feet. He hobbled up the pathway and into the house. "Claire!" he called.

There was no answer. Shit. Maybe he wasn't so lucky. Maybe he had slipped to some other time.

Daniel hurried to the stairs and climbed them to the second floor. He staggered past the master bedroom and hesitated.

The bedroom was empty. No two-by-four. The body of the other version of Bleeker was gone too. Daniel was hopeful again. He was definitely firmly rooted now in the new time line, but where was Claire?

"Daniel?"

Daniel looked up and saw Claire coming out of the corner room.

There she was. Alive. He could breathe again. "Thank god," he said. Tears streamed down Claire's face as she rushed down the hall and fell into Daniel's arms.

It was done. No more loose ends. Nothing from the past could tear them apart again.

TWENTY

Eileen Cho stood on the porch of the old Waynright house, squinting in the late afternoon sun. She watched as the tow truck driver raised Daniel's pick-up truck on the winch. The squawk of the police radio from a squad car drifted across the yard. The heavy-set Cajun deputy was jotting his final notes. Of course, he wasn't surprised about what had happened; after the call he got two nights ago, he figured he'd be back out here again at some point.

Cho looked away and rubbed her weary eyes. She had driven all night yesterday to get here after she had awakened with an intense feeling of dread. Her worst fears had come true.

Daniel hadn't listened to her. She blamed herself for believing he would move on and let it go. She should have known better.

Now he had gone missing.

There had been a search for him in the bayou for over twelve hours that had turned up nothing. There were plans to resume it tomorrow, but the look on the locals' faces revealed more than what they were saying. People don't go missing for long. Not around here. Eventually some part of them turns up in the belly of a gator or on the shore in the backwoods.

This was how it always was.

Cho turned and stepped back into the house. She pushed through the plastic sheeting in the entrance way and into the living room.

She began to feel like a pawn in a larger game. From the first time she had spoken to Daniel on the phone, it seemed as if fate had arranged all this. She had asked him to come to a house where a tragedy had happened. Cho knew the story—the murdered daughter, the parents returning from a trip to New Orleans to find their daughter dead, then shutting up the house and never returning. They had died of sorrow, the real estate agent had told her. They had lost their only daughter and never had any closure. They died knowing that the murderer had never been brought to justice.

Cho had sensed that she had something to do with Daniel's destiny the first time she had talked to him on the phone. But she had never guessed that she would become the conduit between him and his destiny, or how firmly he would become enmeshed in that ten-year-old murder mystery.

Cho crossed the living room and sat silently on the couch. The shimmering noise of the cicadas outside grew louder as a cloud passed over the low-lying sun. She looked down at Daniel's toolbox by the coffee table. His keys and cell phone were still resting where he had left them.

She knew all the theories the police had were wrong. Daniel hadn't had too much to drink, and he hadn't wandered off into the bayou after dark. Daniel had done what she saw in his eyes that he was going to do.

He had gone back.

Cho focused in on Daniel's keys and considered her next move carefully. In the past, channeling through personal items like someone's keys had enabled Cho to reach across the divide. But this was different. Cho didn't believe death was the divide that separated her from Daniel now. Would there be any risk in opening herself up to quantum forces like the ones in this house?

Cho took a deep breath. It was a risk she had to take. She reached out and picked up the keys.

The effect was instant and intense; a simultaneous shudder of extreme heat and extreme cold shot through Cho. Her eyes closed tightly.

Then, an emotion swept over her. It was strong and unambiguous. But it wasn't at all what she expected.

It wasn't a feeling of loss or sadness.

It was a feeling of happiness.

The intense moment of clarity evaporated as quickly as it occurred. Cho sat for a moment in the stillness, then opened her eyes and placed the keys back on the coffee table.

She exhaled slowly. She now had the answer to the question that she so desperately needed. Wherever he was, Daniel was okay. He was exactly where he belonged.

She felt it.

She knew it.

THE END

www.ingramcontent.com/pod-product-compliance
Lightning Source LLC
Chambersburg PA
CBHW051231210726
48290CB00003B/906